A FORK OF PATHS

A Shade of Vampire, Book 22

Bella Forrest

D1707305

ALSO BY BELLA FORREST:

A SHADE OF VAMPIRE SERIES:

Derek & Sofia's story:

A Shade of Vampire (Book 1)
A Shade of Blood (Book 2)
A Castle of Sand (Book 3)
A Shadow of Light (Book 4)
A Blaze of Sun (Book 5)
A Gate of Night (Book 6)
A Break of Day (Book 7)

Rose & Caleb's story:

A Shade of Novak (Book 8)
A Bond of Blood (Book 9)
A Spell of Time (Book 10)
A Chase of Prey (Book 11)
A Shade of Doubt (Book 12)
A Turn of Tides (Book 13)
A Dawn of Strength (Book 14)
A Fall of Secrets (Book 15)
An End of Night (Book 16)

Ben & River's story:

A Wind of Change (Book 17)
A Trail of Echoes (Book 18)
A Soldier of Shadows (Book 19)
A Hero of Realms (Book 20)
A Vial of Life (Book 21)
A Fork Of Paths (Book 22)

A SHADE OF DRAGON:

A Shade of Dragon 1
A Shade of Dragon 2
A Shade of Dragon 3

A SHADE OF KIEV TRILOGY:

A Shade of Kiev 1
A Shade of Kiev 2
A Shade of Kiev 3

BEAUTIFUL MONSTER DUOLOGY:

Beautiful Monster 1
Beautiful Monster 2

For an updated list of Bella's books,
please visit www.bellaforrest.net

Contents

Prologue: Aisha 1

Chapter 1: River 15

Chapter 2: Ben 23

Chapter 3: Sofia 33

Chapter 4: Julie 41

Chapter 5: Aisha 55

Chapter 6: Julie 73

Chapter 7: Julie 87

Chapter 8: River 103

Chapter 9: Ben 119

Chapter 10: River 125

Chapter 11: Ben 135

Chapter 12: River 143

Chapter 13: Julie 155

Chapter 14: Julie 169

Chapter 15: Julie 193

Chapter 16: Julie 207

Chapter 17: River 215

Chapter 18: Ben 219

Chapter 19: River 225

Chapter 20: River 239

Chapter 21: River 251

Chapter 22: Ben 257

Chapter 23: River 269

Chapter 24: River 275

Chapter 25: Ben 289

Chapter 26: Derek... 297

Chapter 27: Julie 309

Prologue: Aisha

As much as the scene beneath me on the ship's deck chilled me to the bone, even those gaunt, naked creatures couldn't haunt my mind for long.

I dipped into the ocean to rinse off the gunk from the werewolf's corpse that had smeared on me, thanks to whoever had dropped it into the box I'd been trapped in. Then, I had to find my family. I had to discover exactly what had happened to them—if my fear that the Drizans had found them really was accurate.

So I left that monster-infested ship and traveled as fast as I could to The Dunes. My homeland. I had barely spent more than a few seconds at a time there since we'd abandoned it. And even those fleeting visits I'd made were without Nuriya's permission. There was a secret gate in The Dunes—at least, I hoped that it was still secret—that connected to Lake Nasser in Egypt, and it had been convenient for me to pass through.

Now, as I descended into the coal-black desert, I shuddered despite the warm breeze.

I wasn't sure what I was going to do. I still hadn't worked out a plan. I paused, trying to clear away the haze of panic and think logically for a minute.

Think like Benjamin would think. That vampire seemed to have a gift for maintaining level-headedness even in the worst of scenarios.

As I took a moment to breathe, I decided that I ought to check The Oasis before venturing further into jinn territory, just to be sure that Bahir had not raised a false alarm and the uneasy feeling in my stomach about their safety was not just paranoia. So I headed to the nearest portal, dove through, and vanished myself back to our atrium.

I couldn't hold back the tears as I gazed around at our once-beautiful home. Ornaments smashed, doors torn open, gardens wrecked.

"Mother!" I cried out, my strangled voice echoing off the

walls. "Father! Sister! Aunt! Is anybody here?"

My calls were only met with silence.

I drew in a deep breath. It took all that I had to not crumple to the floor and weep until I ran out of tears. The Drizans had taken them.

Now that it was verified beyond all doubt that my instinct had been correct, I left the courtyard and returned to the supernatural realm. To The Dunes. I examined the seemingly empty landscape and then began to move, slowly and cautiously, closer to where our enemies resided. I made myself invisible, though I knew that the Drizans would be capable of sensing my presence without sight... they were like bloodhounds when it came to us. It was a wonder that we had managed to survive for as many years as we had without them discovering our location. I guessed that was thanks to Nuriya's order that we didn't go out much. The vampires and half-bloods who served and lived above us had been the only non-jinn we'd had dealings with in a long, long time.

I was barely breathing as I neared the landmark of the entrance to the Drizans' underground palace—a giant scorpion medallion made of solid gold, fixed in the sand. The sight of it brought back dozens of memories, all of them dark and unwelcome.

What do I do?

I dared approach within ten feet of the medallion before stopping and gazing all around me.

I wasn't even sure what my options were. If I tried to force my way into the Drizans' lair with magic—vanish myself into the lower levels—if, or should I say when, I got caught, my punishment would be much greater for having trespassed without permission. My stomach turned just at the thought of the kind of suffering that they would take pleasure in inflicting on me. But what was the alternative? Knock on the door and hand myself over?

The only way to verify that my family was still living was to travel down to the Drizans' prison, where I guessed they were being kept. Or perhaps the torture chambers, even further down in the palace.

But what would I achieve by it? There was no way I was strong enough to free them by myself, and I had no allies in this land. Even if I did manage to break through whatever shackles they were bound in, I knew enough about the Drizans to not be foolish enough to think that we would make it out alive.

I could have backed away and just tried to save myself at least. But I didn't know a life without my family. What was the point of living with freedom but without the people I loved? I would rather sacrifice freedom than be apart from them any longer, no matter what state I might find them in. At least I would be with them, not all alone... especially now that I no longer even had Benjamin as a companion.

Bending over the scorpion entrance, I knocked.

My heart thundered in my chest as I retreated, expecting to hear the bolts slide open any moment now. What I was not expecting to hear was a male voice behind me. "Who goes there?"

I whirled around to see that it was... Horatio Drizan. Son of Cyrus Drizan. He hovered several feet away from me, a scroll of parchment rolled up in his right fist. Horatio was the youngest prince of the Drizan family. Before my family and I left this place, he and I used to play together as children. I hadn't seen him since, but strangely I didn't have difficulty recognizing him. Although he looked very different now—a handsome young man, tall and well-built, just like his father—I recognized those olive-green, slightly down-turned eyes.

I hurried backward even as he tried to close the distance between us.

He frowned. "Aisha?" he asked, pausing. I was surprised that he recognized me so easily.

"Y-You took my family." I stumbled.

His frown deepened. "My father took your family. Yes."

"Are they still alive?"

He nodded slowly, his eyes fixed on mine.

"What has your father been doing to them?" I breathed, afraid to hear the answer.

At this he glanced away, his gaze averting to the golden trapdoor. "You shouldn't be here, Aisha," he said, his voice lowering.

"I can't leave without my family," I said, tears prickling the corners of my eyes. "Please, have mercy."

"It is my father you should be begging for mercy, not me," he said, eyeing me pointedly and clearing his throat. "But I suggest you leave now, if you place any value at all on your life."

"I can't leave," I repeated, my voice shrill with desperation. "If you will not help me free my family, then take me down into your lair with you—"

A scraping came from the trapdoor. The drawing of bolts.

Before I could even catch a glimpse of who was emerging from the trapdoor, Horatio had hurtled toward me and gripped my shoulders. The next thing I knew, my body was shrinking and I collapsed to the ground. As my hands and feet made contact with the sand, I realized that I no longer possessed the body of a jinn. I had the limbs of a mouse…

or a rat. Horatio had caught me unawares and turned me into a rodent. *Is this what they did to my family too?*

"My apologies, Josiah," Horatio called to a young male jinni who had poked his head through the entrance and was surveying the dunes. "I decided to stay out longer. Go back to what you were doing."

With that, Josiah's head disappeared and the trapdoor shut again. My small body quivering all over, I tried to scamper away, but I wasn't fast enough. Horatio's strong hands closed around my body and he lifted me upward until I was level with his chest.

His green eyes were severe as they drilled into mine. "I meant it when I said that you should leave," he murmured.

His hand tightened around my furry midriff and then our surroundings disappeared. When my vision came into focus again, we were standing near a beach. The sand was still coal black. We were on one of The Dunes' shores.

Horatio set me back down on the ground, near the lapping waves. I made a second attempt to scramble away, but he arrested me with his magic. Then my body started tingling all over and expanding until I had resumed my normal form.

I glared daggers at Horatio. "What are you doing?"

"What I'm about to do is for your own good and in time,

you will thank me for it," he said. "Please, trust me… for old times' sake."

"What? No! Wait! What are you—?"

"I'm banishing you from the land of jinn, Aisha."

Before I could scream out in protest, something heavy and invisible hit me square in the chest, knocking all the breath out of me. I went hurtling backward and then upward into the sky, traveling with speed that I had no control over, as though I had just been fired from a cannon. I went soaring over the waves, and I couldn't even twist myself around to face forward. I was stuck, falling backward, watching helplessly as The Dunes, my old home, shrank to nothing but a small speck on the horizon.

By the time I'd slowed down —again, a result of no effort of my own—The Dunes were completely out of view as I hovered over the ocean.

"Damn you, Horatio!" I screamed, fat tears spilling down my cheeks. "Damn you and the whole lot of your wicked family!"

My whole body shaking with rage and grief, I gazed down at the empty waves rolling beneath me. Horatio had said that he had banished me—and I knew what that meant. His curse upon me would mean that I couldn't even enter The Dunes anymore. As a Drizan, he was powerful enough to cast such a curse.

Still, I tried. I couldn't help but try. I hurried back over all the miles that I had been flung and stopped at one of The Dunes' black beaches. As I attempted to move onto the mainland, I was stopped short, barricaded by an invisible boundary. A boundary that I couldn't break through no matter how much I tried.

Horatio had said that he'd done this to protect me. But protection wasn't what I wanted, dammit! I wanted my family, and I wanted to be wherever they were, no matter how horrible the conditions.

But, as the hours passed, I had no choice other than to accept that I could not reenter The Dunes. And so in the end, after much more crying and screaming and cursing, I did the only thing that I could do: leave.

Maybe with hindsight, I would indeed come to thank that prince for sparing me my family's fate—whatever they were still going through—but right now, locking me out felt like the cruelest act in the world.

My shoulders sagging in defeat, I moved away from The Dunes, further out into the ocean. I drifted over the waves, aimless. I did not know where I was going or what I was going to do. I was just… trying to cope with the pain.

I hadn't realized that I'd backtracked so far until I caught sight of Julie's ship a mile away. Forgetting that it was infested with monsters, I wandered toward it. As I eyed its mast, the ship became nothing but a place to sit and rest. I perched myself among the sails and gazed out with blurry vision at the ocean. *What is going to become of me?*

I could not have known how much time passed as I sat atop that mast. I was barely even aware of the deck below— now mostly cleared of the writhing bodies, and standing ones for that matter. They were all, I guessed, packed into the lower decks because this ship was still on a course.

My body felt weaker and weaker as the hours passed. I was starved, but that was not the cause of my increasing frailty. Grief and mourning could weaken jinn and cause their powers to diminish. I'd never experienced such sorrow before, and so had never experienced this phenomenon. It was unnerving feeling my strength ebb out of me. I had to regain control over my emotions, but I simply didn't know how. Soon it felt like it was all I could do just to maintain a grip on the mast and keep myself from tumbling down to the deck.

Anxious to test how much power I'd lost, I dared to move away from the mast and floated directly over the deck. I didn't fall, but it was an unsettling struggle to keep myself afloat. I hoped that I still possessed the ability to transport myself to other places, too.

Though Horatio had told me that my family wasn't dead, who knew how long it would take for Cyrus to get fed up and murder them all? He was an unpredictable man, as unpredictable as an untamed dog.

And Benjamin. *Where is he now?* If all had gone according to Julie and the Elder's plan—and I could not imagine why it wouldn't have—Benjamin would now be completely under the control of Basilius. The vampire would be his puppet, his faithful slave. I hated to think about what was happening to that vampire now, but I knew that I wasn't strong enough to venture back to Cruor by myself. That place had an aura that drained a jinni's soul.

I would only be able to do the bare minimum now, like transporting myself. I could practically feel my powers leaving my bones. And it would remain so until I recovered from my grief.

If I ever recover, I thought with a despairing sob.

It was only once a small island came into view and the pale, skeletal creatures began scuttling around on the deck that I snapped back to the present. It became evident after a few seconds that the monsters were indeed headed for this small island. The vessel began to slow.

The sharks that pulled this boat were fast—and it

seemed that the pale creatures had enough intelligence to be able to navigate. It wasn't long before we had arrived at the beach.

The silhouette of the dark island was very small. It took a few moments to realize what this place was. This was a small, restover island for travelers—similar in concept to The Tavern. Except I'd thought that this island was abandoned many, many years ago. A vengeful dragon had burned the whole place down in his fury. I hadn't known that a new settlement had sprung up in its place. Although the island was nowhere near as developed as it had been before the dragon scorched it, there was still a surprisingly large number of buildings. I wondered how many residents this island sheltered now.

There was a thud. One of the creatures had lowered the gangway and they all swarmed down it onto the beach. They began loping with alarming speed over the sand, swarming together like a pack of wasps. They were heading for the town, or so it seemed.

Soon, there wasn't a single creature left on the ship, and the last of them disappeared into the line of trees that bordered the beach. My skin tingled as a scream pierced the night several minutes later. Then another scream. And then another. Screams that twisted my gut in knots.

Oh, dear. This is not good.

This is really not good.

Chapter 1: River

I ran across the mountain plateau as a wave of fire surged behind me. I'd been running for too long. My legs felt weak. The edge of a cliff came into view. A rickety old rope bridge linked this mountain peak and the next, about half a mile away. I stepped onto the first creaking slat.

The fire was still chasing me. Its heat licked my ankles, sending me hurrying forward. I dared not look down at the terrifying drop. God knew how many thousands of feet were beneath me. I just had to keep forging ahead, and—

One of the slats gave way. I lurched downward in a free fall, stalling myself at the last moment by grabbing hold of one of the ropes that formed the base of the bridge. But my palms were sweaty. I was rapidly losing my grip.

No!

My right hand slipped off, and just as my left began to slide, an arm shot down from nowhere and a hand latched onto my forearm. Then a second hand came down. Strong arms hauled me upward, through the gap and back onto the bridge. Trembling with shock, I found myself standing face to face with... Ben. His green eyes glistened in the glow of the fire, and his skin appeared paler than I'd ever seen it... almost translucent. His hands slid down my arms and he held my hands.

Then he turned around and, keeping me close behind him, began leading me along the bridge, away from the fire and toward the other side. As we reached the lush, grassy plateau, the bridge collapsed behind us and tumbled into the gorge below.

I gazed at Ben in wonderment.

"How did you get here?" I asked breathlessly.

He reached a hand beneath my chin and tilted my head up. His lips brushed against mine in a slow, tender kiss.

"What matters is that I'm here," he replied, his voice deep.

I didn't understand where he'd come from, but I didn't need to. His touch was the only thing I needed, his presence what my soul ached for.

"Will you stay with me now?" I asked.

A flicker of pain crossed his face, and as he looked down at me, there was a sadness in his gaze. A sadness I didn't understand. A sadness that disturbed me. He dipped down and kissed my cheek before saying:

"I'll stay with you... for as long as you need me."

I woke up in a cold sweat, gasping for breath. My eyes shot open, reality returning to me.

I was still in the hunters' submarine. Still bound by my wrists and ankles. Still trapped.

I wasn't sure how I'd even managed to fall asleep in the first place. There must've been something in the tranquilizer they'd shot me with. And how long had I been sleeping? There were no clocks in this room. *How far away am I now from The Shade?* The thought sent shivers down my spine. It felt like the submarine was still moving.

Now what?

Gathering my bound ankles and wrists together, I inched closer to the wall until my back was against it. I stared around the bare room. Fluorescent light strips glowed above me. Everything around me appeared to be made of steel—the door, the walls, the bed frame—giving the cabin a pristine feel. As depressing as it looked, I couldn't fault the hunters for their hygiene. The room almost felt like... an operating room.

What did these hunters want with me? I didn't understand it. When one of them had spotted me in the waves and pulled me aboard his boat, I'd expected him to try to kill me, same as had happened during my last encounter with the hunters. I had been hit by one of their bullets. I likely would've died if not for Ben saving me. But now they wanted to keep me alive. *What for?*

As the cobwebs of sleep lifted from me, I realized what had brought me to consciousness. I needed to pee. *Great.* I scanned the room. Aside from the main door, there was another narrow one that led to a cramped bathroom. Using the toilet with my hands and feet bound like this would be no easy feat. I rolled off the bed, hitting the floor with a grimace. At least I'd managed to land on my side and avoided banging my head too badly. Stretching out my legs and arms, I crawled to the bathroom and awkwardly went about my business.

As I was drying my hands, a key clicked in the front door. Dropping the towel, I froze. The door swung open. In stepped a tall, wiry man clad in black pants and a long black polo shirt. His short-cropped, coal-black hair accentuated his pale complexion, and his face was just as narrow and angular as the rest of his body. With a shadow of stubble around his jawline, he appeared to be quite young—I would have guessed in his early thirties. I recognized this man. I'd caught sight of him on the speedboat as the other hunters had carried me as a prisoner to the lower deck.

Clutched in one of his hands was a small, silver gun, and in the other was a syringe. He eyed me before gesturing toward the bed. "Take a seat, please," he said.

I remained glued to my spot. "Why did you take me?" I asked, my throat feeling drier than the Sahara desert.

"Take a seat," he repeated calmly.

He didn't have the build of a soldier or a fighter—he had more the build of a scientist—but despite the slightness of his physique, there was something imposing about his demeanor. I didn't want to test his willingness to use his gun.

In my move to obey, I forgot that my feet were tied. I tripped and fell, my elbows grazing the metal floor. He tucked the syringe into his pocket, though he kept hold of the gun as he moved to my side. His free hand grabbed my shoulder and he tugged me upward. As he helped me toward the bed, his grip was surprisingly strong.

Once I was seated on the thin mattress, he stepped away and retrieved the syringe from his pocket.

"Are you going to kill me?" I blurted, wincing internally

at how stupid and desperate the question was.

He shook his head, even as he reached out and pressed the end of the gun against my neck.

"Not if you cooperate," he said. "You're too interesting a specimen to kill."

He positioned the needle against my right wrist. I flinched at the sharp prick. I expected him to inject me with some other kind of tranquilizer, but this time, he didn't seem to be injecting anything into me at all. Rather, he was withdrawing blood. Once the syringe was filled, he pulled it from my flesh. Reaching into his pocket, he removed a piece of crisp white tissue which he rolled around the needle. Then he backed away, his gun still aimed at me.

"Then why did you try to kill me before?" I persisted.

He raised a brow. "Before?"

"In Egypt, in the Sahara desert," I said. "You had men stationed there, and the moment they realized I wasn't human, they attacked me."

"Ah, Egypt," he said, nodding his head. "That would explain it. The training of our troops there isn't yet complete, and they're not proficient in distinguishing the varying… degrees of vampirism."

He reached the door and twisted the handle.

"Wait!" I called. "Before you leave, at least tell me what

you want with me."

The corners of his mouth twitched upward in a quick, artificial smile. "You'll find out soon."

CHAPTER 2: BEN

I was on edge every moment that hunter remained in the room with River. As he raised his gun to her before taking a sample of her blood, I was terrified that he was going to kill her. I still couldn't be certain the man was telling the truth about not wishing to kill her, but the hunters' actions so far indicated it to be true. Back in Egypt, after we had first escaped from The Oasis, the hunters' tracking device had picked up on River. They had opened fire because they had just assumed that she was a vampire and hadn't even given her a chance to explain herself. I wondered if this was the first time that this group of hunters had come across a half-blood. From the intense look of interest in this hunter's eyes as he looked at River, I guessed that it was.

But whatever they claimed to want to do, or not do, to River, I couldn't bring myself to believe that their intentions in capturing her were anything but sinister.

After he left the room, River became less tense. She leaned back against the wall again. He still had not unbound her, and it pained me to see how uncomfortable she was beginning to get, being so restricted in her movement. I moved to the wall opposite her and sank down to the floor, my knees bent. I stared at her, recalling her last dream that I'd managed to enter. She must've been wondering where all these random dreams involving me were coming from.

As I'd kissed her in her last dream, I'd been tempted to tell her the truth about what I was, what I had become. She might not even believe it if I told her that I was a ghost—she might discount it as just a stupid dream. But after she'd already witnessed the validity of the previous dream she'd had involving me, I doubted she would dismiss it quite so easily, no matter how hard my words were to accept.

I would sit her down in a future dream and start from the beginning. Tell her everything that had happened to me since I sent her away with Corrine... But now wasn't the time. I couldn't drop that kind of bombshell on her when she was still a captive of these hunters, with no idea what their true intentions were for her. Right now, the only thing I had to set my mind on was figuring out how to help her escape.

If I was to have any chance of saving her, I had to discover where they were taking her. At the moment, the only plan I had was to find out their destination, then return to The Shade and try to get through to someone via a dream. A witch would need to come to save River—it would be too dangerous a task for anyone else… except perhaps for the dragons, but they were too large and cumbersome for this kind of task. I wanted someone who could appear and swipe River discreetly, without causing a huge commotion and turning the mission into a fiery massacre.

I had already briefly explored the submarine, but I hadn't been able to figure out from any of the hunters' conversations exactly where we were headed. So right now, there was nothing I could do but sit and wait with River until we arrived at the hunters' destination.

River let out a deep sigh and leaned her head back against the wall. She stared up at the ceiling, her throat stretched and exposed. I moved toward her and, hovering my hands over the mattress on either side of her, I leaned down and kissed her open neck. At least, I tried to kiss it.

I moved away from her and returned to my previous spot

on the floor. I watched River for the next several hours like she was a movie. I took in every expression that crossed her face, her movements as she tossed and turned on the bed in an attempt to find a comfortable position. Eventually, she curled up beneath the blanket and closed her eyes. Taking her cue, I closed my own and I prepared myself to walk into another one of her dreams. It took a few hours, but eventually one came along…

The sounds of chattering and clinking cutlery filled my ears. A joyful scene unfolded before me—a cozy dining room, filled with people sitting around a long table. River—wearing a pretty blue dress, her long hair flowing down her back and shoulders— was sitting surrounded by her immediate family—Nadia, Lalia, Dafne, Jamil… and a man I was certain was her father. I could see similarities in his features to River's, and Jamil wasn't far from a spitting image of him. Her father's face looked worse for wear—I didn't know his exact age, but I was certain that he looked older than he was—while the rest of his appearance was smart and crisp. He wore a formal suit and his gray-speckled hair was neatly swept back.

Further up the table were humans I'd never met or seen before. Perhaps they were friends or more relatives. As I moved toward the table, River spotted me, her eyes growing wide with surprise. She smiled and leapt up from her chair. Grabbing my hand, she requested Lalia and everyone else to move up a seat to make room for me next to her.

Her face was radiant as I stood with her. She leaned closer to me and, reaching a hand to my face, pressed her lips against my cheek. I didn't even have time to respond before she cleared her throat and looked around the table. Her right hand slipped into mine and squeezed it tight.

"This is Ben," she announced. Her gaze fell on the tall wiry man sitting next to Jamil—her father. Remo was his name, if I remembered correctly.

River was breathless with excitement, her eyes sparkling as she looked from her family and friends to me.

"It's a pleasure to meet you," I said, my voice slightly hoarse as I eyed the strangers.

River's father stood up and reached his hand across the table for me to shake. I gripped it. He flashed me a smile, nodding approvingly. Nadia looked fondly at me, and all the others greeted me with similar warmth.

Then River raised her left hand—which till now had been hidden, tucked in the folds of her dress. Gasps swept around the room. She was wearing a delicate silver ring, encrusted with an emerald-green gem.

"You got engaged?" Lalia blurted through a mouthful of pie, gazing in awe at River's ring.

River beamed and nodded, her turquoise eyes meeting mine. My voice caught in my throat.

"When are you getting married?" Dafne asked from across the table.

River faltered. She ran a tongue over her lower lip and glanced at me tentatively. "We... We're not sure yet." Everyone's gaze turned on me, as though they were expecting me to answer the question.

I was lost for words. An ache filled my chest and suddenly, I couldn't even bear to look River in the eye.

I opened my eyes. The harsh lights of the cabin returned. I glanced at River. She was still asleep on the mattress, continuing her dream without me. Though a slight frown now marred her face.

I didn't know why I felt so shaken by the dream, but I hadn't been able to stand remaining in it a moment longer. I stood up and began pacing the room, my mind agitated, an ache still in my chest. What had disturbed me about it so much? River had been holding my hand. I had felt her lips against my cheek. I'd been touching her. I should've wanted to stay in that dream for as long as it lasted, and yet I hadn't been able to leave soon enough.

After several minutes of prowling, my emotions began to

unravel.

Since becoming a ghost, I had barely thought beyond a few days into my future. I'd just been trying to take things one step at a time. Leave Cruor, find a way back into the human realm, find The Shade… And then when I'd arrived on the island, my mind had been immediately consumed by the chaos that was going on—Jeramiah's plan to finish off my parents and grandfather. Then River had been taken by the hunters. I'd followed her and until now, the time I'd spent on this submarine had been filled with nothing but anxiety over her predicament—a predicament that I was ultimately responsible for.

The scene that I had just witnessed in River's dream… It should've been one of the most ecstatic moments of my life. But it had been nothing but torture. Like someone twisting a screwdriver through my heart.

And it came like a splash of ice-cold water. Experiencing that scene so vividly, as if it had actually been happening, had sent my mind and emotions into a tailspin.

Meeting River's friends and relatives. The ring. Being engaged to River. It was everything that would never happen. A moment that River and I would never share.

A glimpse of a life that we would never lead.

For Christ's sake, I'm a ghost. A damned-to-hell ghost.

I could never be with River. I *would* never be with River. Dreams like that were nothing but a torment for the both of us. When I'd first walked into the dream, the scene had appeared to be a regular family reunion, and if River had not spotted me, I doubted that it would've taken the turn that it had. I guessed that her fantasy would have revolved more around having her father present—presumably out of jail—and all of her family sitting together around one table. It was only my deciding to intercept her dream that caused it to morph into something torturous.

I gazed at River's face, which now bore a clear expression of disappointment. Disappointment that I'd abandoned her, no doubt. Maybe she even took my leaving as a rejection.

I found myself drifting out of her cabin and into the empty corridor. Sitting on the floor, I stared unfocused at the opposite wall.

I didn't know what would ultimately become of me—I didn't possess the emotional fortitude to think of it right now—but there was one thing I knew for certain: I had to stop haunting River's dreams. It was utterly selfish. I had to limit myself to only entering her dreams if there was something that I urgently needed to communicate to her. And even then, I couldn't give in to the urge to turn it into a love scene by kissing or embracing her. In fact, I ought to refrain even from touching her.

In the meantime, I would keep my promise.

I would stay with River for as long as she needed me. And, with all that I had, I would fight to bring her back to safety.

CHAPTER 3: SOFIA

When the dragons, Aiden, Derek and I returned to the island, it seemed that Amaya's spell of sleep had worn off everyone. We spotted crowds of people walking about in a daze, bewildered as to what had just happened. Apparently Amaya's spell hadn't been strong enough to persist for long—just long enough for them to swipe Derek, Aiden and me from The Shade.

I yelled for Corrine and Ibrahim as I spotted them.

"Sofia? Derek? What's happening?" Corrine asked, rushing toward us with Ibrahim.

I explained what had transpired before drawing their attention to Jeriad, who needed urgent medical attention.

Corrine hurried to his side. The shifter was still groaning in agony, one hand clamped over his injured eye. I feared Amaya's curse might have sunk past his eyeball and penetrated the inside of his head. I prayed that Corrine would be able to fix him and he wouldn't become permanently blinded.

Jeriad was in so much pain, he appeared to be bordering on unconsciousness. Corrine and Ibrahim looped their arms through his and supported his weight. They were about to turn their backs on us and head to the Sanctuary—by foot of course, for even in his injured state he'd be mortally offended if they transported him by magic—when the shifter grunted, "The girl. Where is she?"

Everyone froze.

"Girl?" I asked. "What girl?"

At first I thought that he might simply want Sylvia, his human lover, by his side, but then he replied, "Benjamin's girl. River."

"What about her?" I breathed.

He winced, clenching his jaw as though it was a struggle just to speak. "She was riding on my back. In all the commotion, I think she must have slipped."

Goosebumps ran along my skin. I locked eyes with Derek. *Oh, no. No, no, no. Not River!*

34

"Where exactly do you think she fell?" I asked, rushing up to Jeriad and gripping his shoulders, momentarily forgetting he was in pain.

He shook his head, frowning deeply. "I-I do not know. Everything happened so fast and our hides are so thick, we can hardly feel what's on us and what isn't." He drew in a deep breath. "It's hard to pinpoint the moment that she slipped off during the struggle."

"We must return and search for her!" I exclaimed, my voice shaking in panic. I hadn't even known River for long, but after all she'd done to help my son, I'd developed a strong maternal attachment for her.

"You need to recover," Corrine said firmly, even as her brown eyes filled with fear. It was true that I was still feeling weak from the sun, but my skin wasn't that bad. I would heal. Right now, my mind was in too much of a frenzy over River. I had wondered how the dragons had known to come. Had she been the one who'd instigated their arrival? Maybe she'd had another strange, prophetic dream. The thought only crushed me further. *She risked her life to help us, and we left her behind.*

As Corrine vanished, leaving Jeriad with Ibrahim, I prayed that she would find River still floating somewhere in the waves near the cluster of rocks, unnoticed by both Jeramiah and the hunters. Because it was possible that either of them could have taken her.

"I hope Corrine will find River before we have to tell Nadia what happened," I murmured.

Ibrahim continued with Jeriad toward the Sanctuary, and we followed—except my father. He backed away from us, avoiding eye contact. "I'll heal on my own," he said, his voice hoarse.

Ibrahim cast us a glance over his shoulder, as if wondering whether we wanted him to wait for us.

"Just go full speed ahead with Jeriad, Ibrahim," I called. "We'll catch up and meet you in the Sanctuary."

I wanted my father to be treated by a witch, but I couldn't bring myself to argue with him. After losing Kailyn, I guessed that he would crave his own space for a long time to come.

Before Aiden left, I hugged him, gently so as to not cause pain to either his or my sensitive skin, and planted a soft kiss on his cheek. "I love you, Dad," I whispered.

He nodded appreciatively and kissed my cheek back, but his mouth didn't crack even the smallest of smiles. Then he turned on his heel and marched away from us, deeper into the dark woods.

I glanced up at Derek's face. His expression was stoic, though his eyes were filled with disappointment. I understood where his thoughts still were.

He cleared his throat as he met my gaze. "I guess it was naïve of me to think that he would be different."

I reached for his hand and held it tight. I raised it to my lips and planted a kiss over the back of it. "Not naïve, Derek," I said, meaning it as I looked into his blue eyes. In truth, I was proud of Derek for even being willing to consider that Jeramiah might not be a replica of Lucas. I liked to think that it was my influence that had made Derek develop a habit of not always assuming the worst in people, and first giving them the benefit of the doubt. Though, as I'd experienced more times than I wanted to count, as much as this mindset led to living with a lighter heart, it could also lead one into pits of scalding hot water. Still, I tried to comfort my husband. "You turned out different from your father. Why couldn't Jeramiah have turned out different from his?"

He grunted. The disappointment in his eyes was eating away at me. *Poor Derek.* I could relate on a deep level to his desire for a strong, connected family because it was something that I'd never had while growing up. My family had been as dysfunctional as one could get—I'd had no siblings and had been cut off from both of my parents, until I'd rediscovered them in rather unceremonious circumstances at the age of seventeen.

Despite the danger Jeramiah had just thrust us into, Derek appeared to have reached a point beyond anger. He was just... sad. And sadness wasn't an emotion that I was used to from my husband, at least not in recent years. His emotions were usually fiery and swung in extremes—whether in anxiety, joy, passion or anger. Rarely had I witnessed him so crestfallen.

I wrapped my arms around his midriff and hugged him. I wanted to say something to comfort him, like maybe Jeramiah would come round in the end, but after our first encounter, I simply couldn't see how it would ever happen. The young man had refused to even listen to us. He wasn't interested in kindling a relationship with his family. He was interested in only one thing, it seemed—maintaining his posthumous, imaginary relationship with his father, while refusing to believe Lucas was anything but a good man who'd been wronged.

I planted a tender kiss on Derek's cheek.

"We don't need Jeramiah," I said softly.

Derek heaved a sigh. "Of course we don't."

And yet the heaviness didn't leave Derek's expression. My comment had been a stupid one, born out of the fact that I couldn't think of anything else to say. Of course we didn't need Jeramiah. But to Derek, having lost both his father and brother before having a chance to come to even the slightest cordial understanding, Jeramiah would have been a way to make the past less painful. Less regrettable.

Derek pressed his lips against my forehead in a kiss, his mind still elsewhere.

"The man needs help," Derek muttered after a pause. His voice now sounded more grounded than before, his expression less distant, as though hauling himself out of his melancholy and planting himself back in reality.

I couldn't argue with his statement. Jeramiah did need help. He seemed mentally unstable.

"But it would appear we're not the ones to offer it," I said.

Derek nodded slowly in agreement. But then a frown twitched his dark brows. I wondered what had flitted through his mind as he grunted, "Hm."

CHAPTER 4: JULIE

After Arletta and I managed to escape from her turned brothers, we drifted in the ocean for hours. I had not been confident that I'd be able to navigate to land before sunrise—especially since we had no boat and were only swimming—but I'd thought that we'd make it far enough at least for The Tavern's shores to come into view. It turned out that I was being naïve. Horribly naïve.

Dawn broke, and my worst fear came to pass. We got stranded at the mercy of the sun's piercing rays. Though we were lucky that it was the middle of the ocean and not the middle of some sprawling landmass. As vampires, we were able to hold our breath for a long time. This ability was the only thing that saved us. We swam deep beneath the waves and stayed there for as long as we possibly could. Although particles of light still reached us through the water, it wasn't nearly as bad as being out in the open. This of course made traveling all the more difficult, because I could hardly bear to do what was required to gain a sense of our direction: rise to the surface.

I couldn't have known how far we were from The Tavern, but when I finally caught sight of a ship in the distance, I heaved a sigh of relief. We sped up and swam closer. The ship was of unusual appearance—far too beautifully decorated with drapes and flowers, and the wood too intricately carved, to belong to any normal wanderer. And it didn't appear to be steered by vampires, due to the lack of covering over the deck. I didn't know who was in the vessel, or whether we would be welcome aboard, but it didn't matter. We just needed shelter from the sun, and we found that beneath the wooden figurehead of an angel at the bow of the ship. We clung onto the rope fender around the hull and huddled together beneath the shade.

We kept quiet and remained unnoticed. Toward the end of the day, a small island came into view—an island that I had never come across before, nor even heard of. It was clear that this ship was headed right for it. It traveled the last stretch of ocean and arrived in a small harbor. There was a clank. It sounded like a ramp being lowered. Arletta and I had to lean further into the shadow to make sure that we weren't spotted as people began piling off the ship. I soon realized that they were witches, and from the conversations I caught snippets of, they were celebrating a wedding. They were certainly dressed for it. Both men and women were dressed immaculately as they levitated suitcases and bouquets of flowers above their heads.

I couldn't help but wonder why these witches were even traveling by ship when they could easily magic themselves to any destination in an instant. From the way they had decorated the boat, I guessed that the voyage must have been more of a leisure ride than anything else, and now it seemed that they would be continuing the festivities on this little island... It was certainly very picturesque and being quite out-of-the-way—perhaps even unknown to a lot of supernaturals—I couldn't deny that it was a beautiful venue for a wedding.

Arletta and I waited until they had all left the boat and trickled into the line of trees that bordered the beach, and then we waited a bit more until sundown came. Now we could leave the ship without getting burned. We were both starving as we hurried over the beach toward the mainland.

We kept to the trees at first, looking all around us, trying to scope the place out.

Once out of the small forest, we hurried along cobbled streets, winding in and around quaint thatched cottages and square, stone buildings. We kept to the shadows as much as possible. We soon realized that there was quite a mixture of residents here. We spotted some vampires, witches, werewolves, and even a few foul-mouthed harpies. Arletta and I ended up finding refuge for the night in an old shed filled with hay. From the state of it, it appeared to have been abandoned. Our exhaustion drowning out our hunger, we both flopped down against the straw and fell asleep.

The next morning, we had to seriously think about what we were going to eat. Those hours we'd spent fighting to avoid the sun had taken a lot out of us. We managed to find several snakes writhing in the bushes nearby, so those became our meal—our disgusting, but sustainable meal.

In the days that followed, we continued sleeping in the barn. We passed the nights roaming the island, trying to keep our heads down, as we attempted to figure out what we should do next. I couldn't go back to The Tavern—not after the incident involving Benjamin. One of those men who had come to attack Benjamin had survived, and he would no doubt have labeled me a thief and accomplice in his friend's death to the authorities.

Arletta and I spoke surprisingly little considering what we'd just been through together. We were both still in a state of shock, a state of grief. We'd not only lost Hans, but also his brothers, who'd become like my own brothers over the years we'd spent together—witnessing them morph into monsters before our very eyes.

The truth was, I'd spent the last eighteen years waiting for Hans, and I'd never even considered what my life would be like afterwards. I'd just focused on getting through those years without losing my mind. Now I wasn't sure what to do—if there was anything we could do other than try to cope with the grief and mourn the loss of Hans and his brothers.

But as it turned out, our little reprieve was interrupted sooner than we could've expected.

It happened in the middle of the night. Arletta and I were sleeping on a stack of hay when I sat bolt upright, the sound of thundering footsteps filling my ears. Footsteps that sounded like they were coming from just outside. I climbed off the hay stack and swept across the barn to the door. I created the slightest crack with my fingers in the door and peered outside.

I almost screamed. Whipping through the trees all around us were dozens of deathly pale, skeletal bodies. They moved with unnerving speed and from the looks of it, they were all headed straight for the town.

How are there so many of them?

The thought tightened my throat and stole my voice.

Terrified that one could sense us, I closed the door as softly as I could before whirling around to look at Arletta. She was still sleeping on the hay, a peaceful expression on her face, as though all was right in the world. I was afraid to wake her in case she made a sound and attracted some of the monsters to us. At the same time, she couldn't remain sleeping.

I climbed over the hay and kneeled next to her. Clutching her shoulder, I shook her. I still didn't have a plan. I was just working on sheer instinct.

"Arletta," I whispered. "Wake up."

Her eyelids lifted and she looked up at me blearily. "What—"

I pressed a finger to her lips.

"Just come with me," I breathed. "Don't make a sound."

Her eyes widened with alarm at the urgency in my tone and to my relief, she kept her lips sealed. I pulled her away from the hay and the two of us returned to the door. I didn't know where we would go exactly, but we couldn't wait here like sitting ducks. We were just lucky that they were all heading for the town, and didn't seem interested in stopping around here—at least, not the last time I checked...

Shoving Arletta to one side, I planted my fingers along the edge of the door and created a crack, just wide enough for me to peer through.

I let out a slow sigh of relief as I gazed around. It appeared that they had all passed—how many of them had there been altogether? I could hear the sounds of running, many dozens of footsteps, drawing away in the distance. Gripping Arletta firmly by the hand, I pulled her out of the barn and we stepped among the trees.

A shrill scream burst out—a woman's scream, coming from the direction of the town. Seconds later, more screams sounded, and also shouts—male and female alike.

"What is happening?" Arletta gasped.

Still, I wasn't sure if it was wise to tell her. I didn't know if her nerves could take it, if her brothers were once again within close proximity of us.

With all the screams and shouts echoing in my ears, I didn't need to ask myself why they'd come here. But I wondered how they'd gotten here. Had they really managed to navigate the ship all that way? Navigating a ship required skill, intelligence, attentiveness. And in an attempt to numb the pain, I'd been telling myself that there was nothing left of Hans' former self at all. That the monster I'd seen standing before me back in that cave was not my Hans—that my Hans had left this world and moved on to someplace better. That the monster was just an intruder. But the thought that they weren't just mindless creatures—that they possessed intelligence enough to navigate a ship—weakened my desperate theory.

I didn't know what had happened to Hans, but his condition was clearly contagious. While it likely would've taken Hans years to get to the stage we'd found him in, when Hans had bitten into his brother, his brother had transformed within a matter of hours. Now, after the crowds I'd just witnessed rushing through this small forest, their numbers were expanding. Fast. I wondered if the brothers had returned to Cruor to release the others who had been trapped there, Hans included, and now they all ran amok on this small island.

I shoved aside my jumbled thoughts and forced myself to concentrate. Whether or not Hans was here, we had to get out of here without bumping into one of those monsters.

"What is going on, Julie?" Arletta whispered, her voice choked with fright.

I cast her a glare and shushed her before pursing my lips.

I dragged her through the woods, away from the small

barn, until we arrived at the beach. I scanned the length of it and then spotted… my ship. Looming over the shoreline. Yes, they had remained in it all this time, and wherever they had gotten their new recruits, they traveled with them too. Judging from the cries of pain only growing louder behind us, that ship was about to become a lot fuller.

On seeing the vessel, it finally clicked for Arletta what was going on. "Oh my God," she wheezed. "They're here. My brothers."

I nodded grimly. "We need to find a boat and get out of here," I whispered.

I cast my eyes around desperately for any sign of a small boat along the shoreline. I caught sight of a little harbor further up. *Yes.* There must be something suitable there. The two of us raced across the sand toward the harbor and scoped it out quickly to see what would be the best vessel to steal. Something told me that most of the owners of these boats would not be returning for them any time soon.

We picked the smallest boat with the largest engine; three racing sharks, dark teal in color. This type of shark was rare in the supernatural realm—and nonexistent in the human realm—for they were bred by ogres, who made a sport out of shark racing. This boat, however, was too slight of build to belong to an ogre, so I could only assume that a witch, vampire or some other kind of supernatural had found a way to procure these valuable creatures.

I gathered the reins in my fists and tugged hard, stirring the sharks from their resting state. I was about to urge them forward when Arletta let out a gasp behind me.

"Julie! Look!"

I whirled around to face the beach again, straining my eyes to catch what she was looking at. Then I saw, emerging from the line of trees bordering the sand, one of the pale monsters. He was clutching what appeared to be a young woman. Apparently unconscious, she hung limply in his arms as he feasted on her neck.

"What is that woman?" Arletta whispered. "A vampire?"

I tried to make out what the woman was exactly but it was hard from this angle. Although I was quite sure that it wasn't a vampire. Her flesh wasn't nearly pale enough and in fact had a bronzed tone. Perhaps she was a human? Though the chance of there being humans—quite a rare species in the supernatural realm—on this tiny island was slim. As the creature drew closer to the waves with her, I realized that the woman was wearing a wedding dress. Could that be the same happy bride Arletta and I had spied arriving earlier on the island with her entourage? Yes. I was sure that it was.

"Duck down!" Arletta hissed, grabbing my shoulder and

yanking us both down further in the boat. She was right. I had been careless. We should have ducked down the moment we saw that thing arrive at the beach. Both of us dropped lower in the boat, but I kept just high enough to be able to watch what was happening.

Although my brain screamed at me to send the sharks lurching forward, away from this deadly island, my eyes were glued to the pale skeletal figure and his victim. He was surprisingly strong for something so emaciated, who looked like nothing but skin and bone. He held her securely, without her feet even dragging on the ground, even as his fangs continued to tear into her neck, causing a trail of blood in the white sand behind them. They reached the ramp leading up to the Mansons' and my old boat and he boarded it. *Is he turning her into one of them? A witch? No. That would be preposterous. He must just be drinking her blood.* Witch blood wasn't even delectable to vampires, although these creatures were unlike any vampires I'd seen before.

Tears blurred my vision as I thought back to the event that started all this; our encounter with Hans back in the cave in Cruor.

What has become of you, Hans? What has become of us? Of our story?

Where was he now, the real Hans? I still couldn't bring

myself to believe that the creature who had attacked his own brother had been my Hans. How could somebody change so drastically? It was one thing for the physicality of a person to alter, but there wasn't even a sliver of the Hans I used to know left in that body.

As about a dozen more of the creatures burst out from the trees, each of them carrying victims—both vampires and witches—I shook myself to my senses. *What am I doing still stalling like this? Get a grip.* I had to get us both out of here before we ended up the same way.

Tightening my hold on the reins, I urged the sharks forward.

Arletta's eyes were fixed in horror on the beach. She watched as the creatures piled into their ship—our ship— with their newly found victims.

"Keep your head down lower," I ordered her, even as I did the same. Some of them might notice our boat, but hopefully they wouldn't see much more than a seemingly empty boat. The sharks could have gotten fed up of waiting for their master in the harbor.

I needed to navigate us away from their ship, but before I could, thanks to a line of buoys that marked the enclosure of the small harbor, I was forced to swerve outward, closer to the ship. As we moved around the boulders, something caught my eye up in the mast of the ship. Something… someone… was perched there. With long, matted black hair, and a slim body that extended only to the hips before turning into smoke, it was Aisha.

I averted my eyes and focused even harder on racing away from this forsaken place, but she had already seen me.

Chapter 5: Aisha

I'm going to kill that vampire.

The moment I locked eyes with Julie Duan, fury erupted in my veins. So much anger welled within me at the sight of her that it even diverted my mind from mourning the loss of my family.

My body felt weak, weaker than ever, but I left my spot on the ship's mast and glided down toward the two vampires who were now speeding away in their boat as fast as they could. I caught up with them and landed directly in front of where Julie sat, blocking her view of the ocean ahead.

The two vampires froze, panic lighting up their eyes. Abandoning their positions behind the reins, they hurled themselves off the boat and into the ocean. I wasn't going to let them off the hook that easily. I dove in after them, swimming deeper and deeper beneath the surface until I spotted Julie, her legs kicking up a whirlpool as she desperately swam for escape.

Forcing my aching body to move faster, I extended my hands and closed them around the vampire's ankles. She kicked and flailed to break free of me, but slowly, I pulled her back up to the surface. Still clutching her, I tried to lift her above the surface of the waves. To my horror and embarrassment, it was a gargantuan effort to support anyone but myself, and she was only a short woman.

Still, my determination took over and I found a way to lift her. I was greatly tempted to carry her back to the ship, drop her down to the center of the deck, and then return to the mast and watch with satisfaction as the monsters ripped into her. For betraying Benjamin, that was the most fitting punishment that I could think of. Besides, I was feeling too lethargic and weak to keep struggling with the vampire myself. I wanted to hand her over to them and have them finish the job for me.

Then there was the other girl with her... I wasn't sure who she was, but she was clearly an accomplice. Maybe she deserved the same fate too. But she had swum further away, and as I hovered over the waves, I couldn't spot her beneath the surface. I could always come back for her later. Julie was the main culprit. She was the one who was going to feel the bulk of my wrath.

Perhaps it was all my pent-up emotions unleashing all at once in a flood—the grief, fear, hopelessness—but as I carried the flailing vampire toward that ship filled with monsters, something had snapped in me. I felt as bloodthirsty as those creatures.

"No! Please, don't!" Julie sobbed beneath me.

I dug my nails spitefully into her ankle. "You're going to regret what you did to Benjamin, you little bitch. And I'm going to enjoy every single second of it."

There wasn't a single bit of mercy running through my veins as I arrived at the ship and floated with her higher, toward the spot where I'd been perched at the top of the mast. If I'd still been in full possession of my own powers, perhaps I might've concocted a worse way for her to suffer, and a more enjoyable one for me to watch... though I doubted it. But even if I could have, right now, my magic was faded and other than basic movement—which I struggled with considerably—there wasn't much I could personally do to Julie that would be satisfying enough.

I cast my eyes downward, scanning the deck that was now

swarming with the pale monsters again. Their visit to this quiet little island had been brief. I'd watched them all pile off the ship and disappear into the trees, but I hadn't found enough strength or willpower in myself to follow them. My mind had been rooted to the spot, grieving for my family. But then when the creatures had started to return, and I'd noticed Julie trying to escape in her little boat, a surge of adrenaline had jolted me to life, as though I'd just been electrocuted.

Now the monsters were laying out their newly found victims in rows along the deck—the same way they'd positioned their previous catch. Though they had captured a number of vampires, I was shocked to see more than a few witches lying among them. Were these brutes really capable of overpowering witches? Wouldn't the witches have just used their magic to blast them away? Or perhaps the monsters had taken them by surprise, crept up on them in their sleep and dug their vicious fangs into their necks. I guessed that was the more likely scenario—that the witches hadn't even had a chance to retaliate before it was too late. Now that I looked more closely at the victims, the witches were quite still as they lay on the deck, with blood seeping from deep wounds in their necks. They were not displaying signs of consciousness—unlike the vampires who were groaning in pain and writhing about the wooden floorboards.

With Julie still dangling and thrashing beneath me, I knew my hold on her couldn't last much longer. As a vampire, she was strong, and although I still had a little strength left in me, it wasn't enough to keep my grip on the little snake forever.

As what appeared to be the last of the monsters ascended the ramp and arrived on board, I moved closer to the center of the ship where the crowd was thickest. Then, clearing my hoarse throat, I bellowed down, "Hey, folks!"

Each pale face shot upward in unison.

"No!" Julie screamed, her whole body shaking with hysteria. "Please, I beg of you!"

My fingers loosened.

I let go.

She howled as she went plunging downward. But, to my dismay, she did not land where I had intended. The force of her flailing just before I'd let go of her caused her to swerve and miss the center of the crowd. Instead, she fell headfirst into a barrel of water.

Still, it didn't matter. The pale creatures had watched her dive, and were already lurching toward the barrel. One of them turned the barrel on its side, spilling out its water. Julie went skidding across the deck. She scrambled to her feet, gazing all around her in sheer panic. She had nowhere to run. She was surrounded by the monsters, and they were quickly closing in on her.

Her gaze shot to the sails. I already knew what she was going to do. *Dammit.* She leapt upward just as one of the monsters reached out to grab her. She got scraped by his claws and only narrowly avoided his fangs aimed for her neck.

I swooped down on her as she attempted to gain a stronger stance on a wooden boom. I grabbed the back of her neck and whacked her head down against the wood, attempting to bring her into submission. I felt ashamed of how much of a struggle it was to fight with her. If I'd had my powers working at full strength, those monsters would already be feasting on her by now.

Just as I had detached her left hand from its hold and was on the verge of pulling away her right hand, a frigid breeze penetrated my skin. It was so piercing, it felt as though it reached through to my very bones.

I sensed a presence. A cold, dark presence. A presence that made my stomach churn.

I paused, momentarily forgetting my struggle with Julie and allowing her to regain her hold on the boom. I was too preoccupied by the vision unfolding before me on the deck. A strange black mist had settled over it, emerging from nowhere. It swirled and began forming a denser fog.

Even the monsters became distracted from Julie. Those who'd been impatient for me to loosen Julie and drop her down to them had been on the verge of leaping up, but now the focus of each of them was on the black vapor. Their faces were blank as ever, though I could have sworn that I caught a glimpse of curiosity behind them.

The black fog, now so thick that I could no longer see through it at all, took on a reddish tinge. Then came a bone-chilling voice. The voice of an Elder.

"Children," it hissed. It was addressing the monsters, I could only assume. *Could they even understand it?*

The dark, fluid smoke dipped down and engulfed the nearest creature to it. *The Elder is attempting to inhabit him.* The monster let out a guttural snarl and began shaking his head violently from side to side. He dropped to the floorboards on all fours, arching his back like a cat, his hissing and snarling intensifying. A moment later, the Elder reappeared. The black fog drifted out from the body and floated upward. The Elder let out a long, agitated hiss. Its attempt to possess the monster had apparently gone in vain.

There was a pause, and then the smoke moved down

again, attempting to consume a different creature this time. But as before, the Elder was expelled after barely a few seconds had passed.

Who was this Elder?

Based on the noises it was making, it was growing more and more angry and frustrated. Then it stopped trying to enter the creatures' bodies and instead drifted higher, until it arrived at Julie's level. Just as I'd been frozen in my spot, Julie had also been gaping at the Elder. It would have been wiser for her to use this distraction to attempt to escape, but it seemed that she was too taken by the scene to think of it.

Now that the Elder had arrived right next to her, her face grew paler than it already was, if that was even possible. She gaped at the Elder's ethereal form.

"Basilius?" Julie breathed.

"You failed me, girl." His voice turned to ice.

"I-I'm sorry," she stammered, her knuckles stark white as they gripped the boom.

Basilius moved closer to her, and before she could even leap away, his mist enveloped her body. Her eyes bulged and her lips parted, shock flashing across her face. And then the Elder emerged again, almost as fast as he had apparently been forced to exit from the monsters beneath us. "You see," Basilius continued, "the Novak boy was our only hope. He was the one I was meant to inhabit and now he is lost to us forever."

"What?" Julie and I gasped at once.

"The vial," he hissed. "He drank from the vial you left in his pocket. His body is now useless! He is dead!"

Benjamin. Dead. The words hit me like a punch in the gut. My already wrecked heart had just been ripped further.

And what vial? I hadn't even been aware that Benjamin was carrying a vial. He'd never mentioned it to me... then again, he'd never talked to me much. He only ever spoke to me when he needed to.

Did he really commit suicide?

Despite the way he shoved aside my advances and made it painfully obvious that he neither liked me nor wanted me around, I couldn't help but become attached to him during the time we spent together. I might have even loved him. Tears heated the corners of my already sore and bloodshot eyes.

"You see that I cannot inhabit you—a regular vessel," the Elder continued his chastisement of Julie. "Or even the Bloodless."

The Bloodless? I gazed back down over the pale creatures. *That's what the Elders call these things?* I eyed their stark white skin. They certainly looked bloodless.

"What are the Bloodless exactly?" Julie asked, feebly, jerking her head down toward the creatures who were still distracted, staring at the Elder.

I wasn't sure what made the Elders think that they could inhabit the Bloodless, if they weren't even strong enough to inhabit regular vampires. If what Basilius had just told us was really true—that Benjamin was gone—this Elder was running only on the strength he'd built up during the time that he was able to gain sustenance from Benjamin's blood consumption. I guessed that this leftover strength was the only reason that he was even able to travel to this ship. Evidently, they were desperate. They must have hoped that this strange species of monster would be easily inhabitable by them... their natures were certainly infused with the same evil.

Now their hopes had been dashed to the ground. Whatever these dark creatures were, at least the Elders weren't able to inhabit them. Due to Basilius' bond with Benjamin, the Elder had been able to influence and gain strength from him, but with Benjamin dead, it seemed that the Elders truly had lost their final hope of a resurgence. For without vessels even one of them could inhabit, they had no means of procuring new blood or resuscitating themselves.

"What are these creatures?" I asked the question a second

time, for Basilius had still not answered Julie. Of course, the Elder had no reason to reply to a jinni, or to Julie, considering how angered he was by her. The fury in his voice was almost tangible. Julie was lucky that he was too weak to occupy her, otherwise I was sure that the punishment he would have meted out on her would have been hell. Maybe even on par with vampire-zombies ripping into her.

Still, the question plagued my mind. *What exactly are the Bloodless?*

The Elder refused to answer. With another hiss of frustration, he jerked away from Julie and began whirling round and round the ship before he vanished. Almost instantly the temperature became warmer again, and the pleasant, mild breeze returned. As though someone had just flicked a switch, Julie, the monsters and I resumed the positions we'd been in before the Elder's interruption had paused time.

Julie began to scramble further up the mast, away from the Bloodless below as they once again set their dull eyes on her. I hurried toward her. Grabbing hold of her arm, I slowed her down in her ascent.

"No! Aisha, listen to me. Please, you must! I-It's what Benjamin would've wanted."

Playing the Benjamin card was the very worst thing she

could have done. My fury reached a boiling point. Raising my hand, I backhanded her in the face. "How dare you even utter his name!" I seethed.

"Unless we do something about this infestation, it is going to spread!" Julie panted, her eyes wild and desperate. "We're the only people who know about them, the only people who are here…" Her voice trailed off as one of the Bloodless reached her level on the mast. Kicking hard, with one swift motion she dove off the ship and landed with a splash in the waves. I shared a grunt of frustration with the Bloodless who'd just swung for her and followed her down as the rest of the monsters also corrected course.

Hovering over the foaming waves, I plunged my hand into the water and caught her ankle before she could get too deep. I tugged her up to the surface. Gripping her by the shoulders, I hauled her into the air.

"Aisha," she gasped. "The Bloodless are going to continue to multiply. What don't you understand about that? We're the only witnesses alive who can do anything about it. Please, we need to work together, at least until we've gotten rid of them. If we let them go, the supernatural realm is going to become flooded with these monsters! We have a responsibility!"

I didn't trust a word coming out of her lips. Yes, we were

the only ones around with the power to do something about this before they expanded further—which did seem to be their plan—but I didn't believe for a moment that even a single bone in her body was genuinely concerned for the wellbeing of her fellow residents of the supernatural realm. Not after she had so viciously betrayed Benjamin. This was just a pathetic attempt to save her neck, and citing our responsibility to deal with these monsters was nothing but an excuse to delay her demise.

She squirmed harder as I dragged her back toward the ship.

"Please, Aisha! These creatures are dangerous not only to vampires. Didn't you see that they killed dozens of witches? What's to say they're not a threat to jinn too? We need to—"

"There is no *we*," I growled. "Even if I wanted to spend my time acting for the greater good of our supernatural realm, I don't need your help. I can do it by myself."

Of course, that wasn't entirely true. In fact, not really true at all. I could manage basic movement, and could just about carry Julie because she was only small and light in weight—although even that was a struggle when she squirmed fiercely—but taking on an entire ship filled with these creatures would be too strenuous without command of my full powers. Julie would have been of use, in fact, but I would sooner see the entire supernatural realm infested with these nightmarish creatures than accept this wench's offer of help.

"Aisha, I'm sorry," she continued to plead shamelessly.

"Oh, I'm certain that you're sorry. And you're about to become a lot sorrier."

"Two wrongs don't make a right!"

"My math works differently."

"No! Please, let her go!" a female voice shrilled behind us.

Annoyed by yet another distraction, I turned to see the girl who had been traveling with Julie in the boat before she'd jumped into the waves and escaped from my sight. Now she swam toward us in the ocean, terror gleaming in her eyes as she looked from Julie to me.

"Please," she said frantically. "Have mercy. Don't kill Julie. I can't survive without her. I've lost everyone!"

"And do you think you're the only one who's lost everyone?" I roared, a wave of anger and grief surging in my voice.

The three of us fell silent as I took in a deep breath, attempting to regain composure.

Then Julie spoke, her voice quieter and calmer this time. "The way to honor Benjamin is not through revenge."

I couldn't believe the gall of her as she craned her neck up to look me in the eye.

"The way to honor him," she continued steadily, "is to ensure that the sacrifice he made does not go in vain. He wanted to keep our worlds free from the Elders, and prevent countless more innocent people from suffering by their resurgence. He sacrificed his life to ensure a better one for the rest of us and, although the Elders might be out of the picture now, we must tackle these creatures. Can you imagine the type of havoc that could ensue if they ever found a way into the human realm? That has been your home for the past decades, has it not?"

It still irked me to no end that she was using Benjamin's name to get herself off the hook, but her words had struck a chord in me. No matter how pained I was to admit it, I couldn't deny that her words were true. Benjamin had sacrificed himself to protect the lives of others. If we just sat here and did nothing while these Bloodless slaughtered entire islands, how would that be honoring his memory?

I gazed reluctantly down at Julie. I could see behind her eyes that she was using up every one of her last prayers to beg that this new approach would work on me. It didn't work because I trusted her or her motives, it worked only because I knew it was what Benjamin would have wanted.

The ship was packed with Bloodless and they were

expanding fast. Still, we were in the unique position of being able to do something about it while we were at sea again and all of them were contained in the same boat. We just had to find a way to slaughter these creatures, and then—unless monsters like this had already sprung up in other parts of the supernatural world—the infestation would be halted. And I could not do this alone. I was still in the grip of my emotions over being cut off from my family, and I would need help.

"Where are your other accomplices?" I asked, frowning.

A pained expression crossed Julie's face, and by the intensity of it, I believed her to be genuine when she replied, "We lost them."

From inside the box, it had sounded like the others had been men. If they were indeed all lost, that left only Julie and this other girl who'd been a part of Julie's deception. I averted my eyes to the second girl, looking her over. Julie and I could manage this mission... and I was still unsatisfied.

Dropping Julie into the waves, I darted for the second girl. She appeared so shocked that she barely even had time to react. Clamping my hands around her throat, I lifted her up. I was pleased that she was thin and wiry in build, and she seemed overall weaker than Julie, so she wasn't too difficult for me to lift. Bringing her to the ship and hovering back over the deck, I did what I'd been dying to do for what felt like the past hour.

I tossed the vampire into the swarm of salivating Bloodless, and then watched, relishing the girl's screams.

The Bloodless piled on top of her, digging their fangs into any part of her that they could reach. They appeared to be ravaging her much more severely than any other vampires I'd watched them sink their teeth into. Perhaps it was all the buildup they'd just endured. Three latched onto her neck at once, while others were forced to resort to other parts of her body; her arms, wrists, stomach…

Julie was screaming at the top of her lungs, still down in the ocean, but her shrills merged into the background. *Just be happy I chose her instead of you, bitch.*

My face hardened as I watched the Bloodless swarm like wasps around the vampire. Watching her demise was gruesome, yet utterly satisfying. Like scratching an itch that had been plaguing me for weeks.

I waited until the Bloodless had stopped drinking from her, and laid her punctured, blood-soaked body on the deck, where she began trembling—her new transformation apparently underway. I had just created one more problem for Julie and me to eliminate, but, oh, was it worth it.

I hovered back over the edge of the ship and arrived above

Julie. She bobbed in the waves, rigid with shock and horror.

I narrowed my eyes on her. "Annoy me, or step out of line even once, and the same fate will befall you."

Chapter 6: Julie

Arletta!

I was still in a state of shock. Hans' siblings were the only family I had, and I'd just lost all of them within days. There wasn't a single Manson left standing. As tiresome as Arletta could sometimes be, she was like my own sister. Now, I had no one at all. I was too shaken to even cry.

The jinni swooped down once again and roughly gripped my shoulders. She hauled me out of the water and lifted me, giving me a bird's eye view of the vessel. It was still too early for me to feel hatred for the jinni. I just gaped in disbelief over what she'd just taken from me.

A part of me now almost wished that she had dropped me

into the crowd of Bloodless after all. At least I wouldn't be alone. I'd be with the Mansons, no matter how horrific it would be.

Maybe Braithe, Frederick, Colin, Arletta and I could even make our way back to Cruor in our monster forms and be united with Hans again. I guessed that Cruor was where Hans must have still been, because I hadn't spotted him here. At least Frederick, Braithe and Colin were still among the crowd, and Arletta would soon join them. It was a lance through my heart to see the brothers' faces, once so handsome, just like their older brother, now deformed into these abominations.

I shook myself.

Stop thinking with such finality. There's got to be some kind of cure, even if it only makes them half the people they were before. There's just got to be.

I was shaken from my thoughts as the Bloodless began snarling and leaping up toward me and Aisha, who had started floating toward one of the ship's masts. The jinni's hold on me was gut-wrenchingly loose, and I was terrified that she was going to change her mind and drop me down into the crowd after all. Especially when a strong gust of wind swept up, adding to the precariousness as it rocked me from side to side.

"So what has your little mind come up with regarding how to get rid of these things?" Aisha asked me.

It was a struggle to even find my voice, still aggrieved by what Aisha had done to Arletta. I still wanted to be silent, left to my own thoughts, but being dangled over a ship of ravenous bloodsuckers had a way of making one find one's voice in even the most difficult of situations.

"They can't be killed like normal vampires," I stammered, clearing my parched throat and trying to steady my voice. "I watched one get stabbed before, right through the chest. The weapon pierced his heart, but he didn't die. I don't know how to kill these things." *Or even if they* can *be killed.*

There was a span of silence as the jinni surveyed the deck. "Curious," she muttered to herself. "Well, I would like to witness this for myself. You'll try it again, and if it doesn't work, you can always try severing the head—"

"Wait... Me? I can't do this all by myself. That's why I said that we need to work together."

"I meant what I said," Aisha replied, an infuriating smile spreading across her face. She gazed down on me with spiteful contentedness. "You're going to be our guinea pig. And you're going to keep experimenting until we find a way to kill them. So if you want to save time, and not lose your life in the process, I really suggest that you think long and hard what the best way is to go about this." Her attention snapped back to the ship. "So," she continued briskly, "we need to find you something sharp…"

Oh, God. Is she really going to drop me back down there all alone again? My stomach twisted itself into knots as she began to descend on the deck. I expected her to continue lowering with me, but she leveled us out—frighteningly close enough to the Bloodless' claws, but not quite low enough for them to gain a grasp on me and yank me from the jinni's careless grip. Thankfully, these monsters couldn't leap as high as regular vampires. I looked toward where Aisha was heading—the front of the ship. I realized now that she had spotted the barrel that we kept there—filled with weapons. Daggers, swords, spears, even a few guns. She moved faster as the Bloodless followed beneath us. Arriving at the barrel, she dumped me unceremoniously on the deck.

"So, Julie," the jinni said in a soft, sweet voice—a voice that was entirely at odds with her malicious countenance. "You wanted to honor Benjamin's memory and fight for the greater good of the supernatural realm. Now you've got your chance. Have at it."

My hands trembled as I whirled to face the wave of Bloodless surging toward me. It took all that I had to resist the urge to throw myself back into the ocean. That would do no good. Aisha would merely catch me again and bring me right back to the deck—and, possibly, this would irritate her enough to not even allow me to arm myself. So instead, I did the only thing that I could.

I rushed to the barrel and picked up the nearest two weapons to me—a sword in one hand, a rifle in the other.

Drawing the blade from its sheath, I scanned the Bloodless closest to the front of the crowd to make sure none of them were Mansons. Then I raised both weapons in front of me and began firing the rifle. The bullets had little to no effect. If anything, it only agitated them further and made them speed up. Even when I shot one straight through the head, or in the eye, they continued running regardless. By the time they reached within six feet of me, I had urinated on myself.

Discarding the rifle while cursing it for its uselessness, I grabbed hold of one of the ropes hanging from a mast behind me and managed to elevate myself just in time before one of them could grab my ankles. I climbed as high as I possibly could, perching right at the top of the mast, and gazed down at the Bloodless following me up. At least from this vantage point, I could see them coming and could better angle my sword at them. That, and Aisha could more easily come to my rescue if things got really bad. I had to pray that she would do this for me and not leave me to my fate.

As the first of the Bloodless reached me, I scanned his terrifying face to check once again that he wasn't one of the Mansons. Seeing that he wasn't, I hit him with my sword, plunging it deep into his chest, even though I had already witnessed such a method not doing a thing. Aisha had seemed to doubt me when I'd told her though, so this was mainly to demonstrate to her that I'd been telling the truth. I dared glance upward for a split second, to catch sight of her hovering several feet above me in the air, watching intently.

With a strong thrust of my foot, I kicked the Bloodless in the head, causing him to lose balance and tumble down to the deck... Only to make way for the next one.

This one was stronger and had much faster reflexes. Horrifyingly fast. Before I could even plunge my sword into his body to create a distance between us, he'd leapt at me, his hands closing around my throat. His claws sank in, puncturing my flesh.

"No!" I let out a strangled scream.

Aisha swept down. Grabbing the sword from my hand, she plunged it into his neck—the force of the motion sending him reeling, and also, inevitably, losing his grip on me. He tumbled down to the deck with the others. Sliding one arm around my waist, the jinni jerked me upward. I whimpered as I clasped my hands around my neck. It was soaked with blood, and the wind stung like hell. However, I should've been grateful. His claws hadn't dug into me nearly as deeply as I'd imagined. I guessed that he'd been saving that job for his fangs.

"Thank you," I breathed, barely even aware of what I was saying. I was just so relieved to be carried away.

"Don't thank me," Aisha snapped. "I only saved you because you're still of use to me."

My heart hammered against my chest as she stopped ascending and hovered, still in one spot. She flashed her eyes at me, indicating that I take the sword. I took it from her cautiously, with half a mind to attempt to stab her in the gut and escape this nightmare. But I didn't know if jinn could be killed by stabbing—they were ethereal creatures, after all—and I was too afraid to risk finding out.

"Let's try again, shall we?" Aisha continued, her tone almost bored. "I think we've verified by now that it's not possible to kill one of these things by stabbing them through the chest—or the neck, for that matter. This time, I want you to try chopping off a head."

I choked as she lowered me back down again. This time, she didn't even bother to take me to an empty part of the ship. She just dumped me down on the railing, right next to a crowd of Bloodless. Now I was sure that she intended to kill me. She was just having a little fun with me first. *Curse the bitch.*

They came rushing at me again, and, the hilt of the sword slippery in my sweaty hands, I lunged at a Bloodless' head with all my strength. The edge of my sword sliced through flesh, but then it was met with a dull thud. Metal against bone. Tough bone. Very tough bone. I stared at the Bloodless' wraithlike face. It barely even registered pain. Just hunger for my blood. The sword dislodged and clattered to the floorboards as he lunged at me. I thanked my stars that Aisha had planted me by the edge of the ship. Knowing that the jinni would have been observing my attempt closely, I leapt off the ship before the Bloodless could grab me.

Splashes came from behind me. During previous encounters with the Bloodless, I had noticed that they appeared to be somewhat averse to water, and so I'd hoped that they wouldn't follow me. But it appeared that by now, Aisha and I had riled them up far too much for them to care.

"Help!" I screamed up at Aisha, who was still keeping track of me from above.

I didn't have the nerve to stay above the surface and wait for her to descend. Taking a deep breath, I dipped under the waves and began to swim manically away. But it wasn't long before the jinni's warm hands closed around my calves.

"Trying to escape again, are we?" she drawled, hoisting me into the air.

"No!" I spluttered. "In case you didn't notice, if I hadn't jumped that Bloodless would have torn into my neck."

"Oh, of course you aren't," Aisha replied, patronizingly, as if she were a teacher talking to a school child. "It would be rather stupid of you to try that again after the warning I gave you."

As she was about to drag me yet again to the ship, I craned my neck up to meet her eyes and begged, "Aisha, I don't think this is the best way to do this. I really don't." I gritted my teeth. *I really, really don't.* "I couldn't even cut through that monster's neck with the blade. The bone was hard as a rock."

"Perhaps all we need is a sharper blade," Aisha said, almost nonchalantly.

"Maybe," I said, trying to not spiral into a nervous breakdown at the thought of the jinni dropping me among the Bloodless yet again. "But we're going into this blindly. These are clearly nothing like the vampires either of us know. We need to try to figure out what these things actually are before we have a chance of ending them…" I paused, drawing a rasping breath. "Look, I'm shaking and weak, and if you drop me down there again, I don't think I'll survive. I-I can't handle it."

Aisha paused mid-air. "Aww," she crooned, the fakeness of her concern biting. "Maybe you should've thought about that before volunteering to save the world?"

"Please! This isn't working."

The jinni's expression turned stone cold. "And what do you propose exactly? That I just forget about what you did to Benjamin and let you go free?"

"No," I said, shaking my head fiercely. "You may not believe me, but I meant it when I said that I want to help solve this." My words were true. I wanted to solve this problem… just for a different reason than I'd revealed to Aisha. I didn't want to slaughter them, at least, not Hans' siblings. I needed to find a way to cure them, or find some way to get them back to a state where they were at least semi-recognizable. Hans was still trapped in that dark cave in Cruor, but if I could just figure out how to fix his siblings, it would be a step closer to reuniting with him again. *The real him.*

"I just think that we should know what we're doing before attempting it. Is that so unreasonable?"

Aisha paused, and I even dared get my hopes up that she was considering my words.

"Well, what exactly are you proposing then?" she huffed. "I have a suspicion about what these creatures are, but I'm not aware of how to eradicate them. That's why I said we need to experiment. You don't have a clue about them either, and heck, even the Elder was tight-lipped."

Here, I had to be cautious. I held my breath, bracing myself for her reaction. "I, uh… I think that we should go see a witch."

Aisha's nose wrinkled. "A witch? What witch?"

"I was thinking that we could return to the witch doctor's island… Uma's island. She has vast medical knowledge about all types of supernatural creatures because she treats them. She may not have encountered one of these creatures before, but I'm sure she would have more of an inkling than us about them and how one might be able to kill them."

"I still think decapitation is the way to go," Aisha said, still on edge at the mention of seeking help from a witch. It appeared that jinn and witches were reluctant about accepting help from each other. "It's probably as simple as finding a sharper blade to cut through the bone. We don't need a witch."

"I think we should at least try Uma," I said, desperate to get through to her. "We're not even that far from the island. With your powers, it wouldn't take us a long time to get there."

Aisha shook her head. "That snotty witch won't even see us unless we scout some impossible list of ingredients for her. Seeking her out is a stupid idea."

In my desperation, I'd forgotten about Uma's ridiculous demands. Of course, the witch would expect something in return.

"I-I still think that we should try," I persisted. "If we bring a specimen with us, she might just see that as valuable enough an offering to grant us a visit... I mean, this is an entirely new species of creatures. I'm sure that we would be able to arouse her curiosity enough for her to agree to take a look."

"A specimen, huh," Aisha said, glancing down at me with a frown. Then her expression lightened, the corners of her mouth curving slightly. Somehow, Aisha's smile was far more disturbing to me than her scowl. "Very well," she began slowly, "if you want to gather up a specimen, I'll take you to the witch's island... Let's see how much you really want this."

I gulped, glancing over the bald, white-headed creatures.

I was hoping that the jinni would help me with this at least. But doing it all by myself had at least one advantage...

I could see that Arletta was still in transformation at the

far end of the deck. My eyes shifted toward the main crowd and I scoured the faces in search of Hans' brothers. I spotted Braithe at the forefront, the other two close behind him.

I wanted to take them all with me, but I knew that would be too suspicious.

But I was getting ahead of myself. Before thinking about saving all of them, I had to figure out how to get just one of them out of there.

"I'll need to use the box," I said nervously. "But how? How would I do that without being bitten?"

"Oh, I'm sure you'll find a way," Aisha said nonchalantly. "You have a rare talent for figuring out how to save your own skin."

I felt goosebumps as Aisha lowered me again to the boat, heart-stoppingly close to the Bloodless.

"Okay," I wheezed, trying to force my panicking mind to think clearly. "I will need to search for the box, and I'll try to lock one of them inside and then... then you'll need to help me lift the box away. There is no way that I can do this all on my own."

"Deal," the jinni said. "If you manage to herd one of those things into your blasted box, I'll help you get it off the ship."

Chapter 7: Julie

Mercifully, this time, Aisha lowered me onto the mast instead of the deck, directly above the trap door that led down to the ship's lower levels. The trap door was flung wide open. I couldn't be sure whether or not any of the monsters were down there.

The moment my feet hit the mast, the Bloodless began hurrying toward me. Again I fought my every instinct to leap back into the ocean and swim like a maniac. This time, I would need to dive right into the fray.

Tearing off a piece of sail using my claws, I wrapped it tightly around my throat to form at least somewhat of a barrier against the monsters, no matter how measly. The rest of my body would have to remain as it was—vulnerable and unprotected—because with the Bloodless encroaching, I had no time to come up with more makeshift armor.

With one giant thrust of my legs, I flung myself from one side of the ship to the other. They all hissed and spat, turning to follow. But as soon as they neared me on the other side, I pulled the same trick, moving back to the previous side. I wasn't sure what I was doing. I was flying completely by the seat of my pants, just hoping that my antics would disorient them and place me at some kind of advantage.

But things didn't exactly pan out that way.

The Bloodless wised up, and, rather than follow me from mast to mast, they displayed an unnerving level of intelligence and split into two groups, positioning themselves at each one. I could no longer play this game, especially as the Bloodless began swarming up both of the masts. At least in doing so they left the deck clear. I took the opportunity to leap down and sprint for the trapdoor.

It felt like I was committing suicide as I dove down the stairs. I couldn't even pull the trapdoor shut above me to buy myself some more time. It was broken, splintered to pieces. Landing with a crash at the foot of the staircase, I loped along the hallway toward the small storage room where the box had been kept.

I knew this ship like the back of my hand—it was my ship, mine and the Mansons'—but in my panic, my brain almost forgot my way around. The state of the ship didn't help. *Good grief...* The whole lower deck was horribly disfigured. They'd wreaked havoc, shredding the walls and ceilings with their claws.

My heart was in my throat as their footsteps descended the stairs. I reached the storage room where I'd left the box. A horrid, vile smell filled my nostrils even as I exhaled in relief to find that the box was still here. Its lid was open, and when I hurried up to it, it was filled with the rotting body of a werewolf. I felt nauseous from the stench. *Who put this in here?* I wasn't sure how long the body had been lying there, but it was already riddled with maggots and flies.

Clenching my jaw, I held my breath and dove my hands into the box. Grabbing hold of the thick fur around the wolf's neck, I tugged with all my strength. The body was heavy and bloated, and though I could handle the sheer weight, I was physically much smaller than the beast. I managed to pull it out of the box, but as the body flopped to the floor, it crashed down against my shins and feet. I lost balance on the slippery floor and collapsed onto the werewolf's body, which, to my horror, squelched like a water balloon. A burst of brownish liquid burst forth from the werewolf's mouth and doused me. Although I was trying to keep quiet, I couldn't help but shriek. The corpse's smell was overpowering as it was, and now to be soaked in its putrid body juice...

Footsteps sounded outside in the corridor. I hurtled to the other side of the room and jammed a shelf against the door. That would do nothing to prevent them from entering, but at least it would act as a slight deterrent. The door handle rattled and fists pounded against the door. My blood throbbed in my ears as I turned away from the door to face the corpse of the werewolf again. If my adrenaline had not been raging so much, I probably would've passed out by now just from the smell alone, never mind the crowd of Bloodless about to break in.

My eyes fell on the white box. The "Elder box", as Benjamin had called it.

I've found the box. But now what? I hadn't thought further ahead than this. Aisha hadn't given me the time to. Wood splintered. The pounding was growing heavier and more violent against the door.

Think! I ordered myself, although all I wanted to do was scream.

And then it was too late.

The weight I'd barricaded the door with gave way and the Bloodless began spilling into the storage room.

This was the end. I was a rabbit cornered by a pack of wolves. There was no point in even fighting. What could I do in this tiny room? There weren't even any windows here.

I closed my eyes tight, praying that at least the pain wouldn't be too unbearable. And whatever I emerged as after this, my brain wouldn't have turned into a vegetable....

My whole body tensed as I steeled myself for the monsters' claws to slice my flesh and fangs to sink deep into my neck.

But neither happened.

Daring to open my eyes, I was shocked to see that the Bloodless had stopped still, about three feet away from me. Braithe was near the front of the crowd that had burst into the room. They stared at me, their small eyes fixed on me intently. I didn't know what they were waiting for. And I was even more clueless when the Bloodless began to back away out of the door. As though I'd somehow just become... Uninteresting to them. Unpalatable.

I gazed down at my own form. I was covered in rotten corpse fluid. The smell—obnoxious as it was—could that really have put them off me?

Emboldened by this sudden, unexpected turn of events, I left the room too and cautiously followed them. Braithe had been among the last to leave the room, and now he was the closest to me in the corridor. I didn't know what madness possessed me, or rather what desperation, but I found myself quickening my pace and extending my hand. I reached up and closed it around Braithe's rawboned shoulder.

He let out a hiss and whirled around to face me, his fangs bared, his nose wrinkled in a snarl. My pulse raced, but I did not flinch. I remained rooted to my spot, staring at the abomination who'd once been my lover's brother. Though he appeared agitated, Braithe was still making no move to launch at me.

The other Bloodless who'd been loping down the corridor also turned around to look me over, but they soon got bored of me and turned around. Braithe, on the other hand, stayed watching me longer. I wanted to believe that a small part of him remembered me, but more likely, it was because I had reached out and touched him. After several moments, he also appeared to get bored of me and turned around to follow after the others.

The moment his back was turned to me, I reached out

and clutched his shoulder again. Only this time, I didn't let go. I was sure that I had lost all sanity at this point, but all I could do was act on my raw instinct. He hissed more loudly this time, but on turning around, he still did not attempt to lash out at me. If anything, he looked like he just wanted to squirm away, the way one would shrug away from a hairy spider.

He tried to shake off my grasp again, but I held on tight. My hand slid down his arm and settled around his right wrist. I tugged on him. He was strong—frighteningly strong for a creature of such meager build—and he didn't budge an inch. I pulled on him harder—much harder than I was comfortable with. I managed to move him a bit this time, even as his almost nonexistent lips curled.

Still, I persisted. Grabbing hold of the doorframe, I used it as support to yank harder. This worked. The force of my tugging took him by surprise and he stumbled, losing his firm stance. I managed to drag him back into the storage room, where I slammed the door shut behind us. By now his snarls were becoming growls and as he bared his fangs, I was beginning to fear for my life. If he decided to overlook the scent of the body juice, it would only take one bite to discover my blood underneath...

I had to move faster. He was close to the box now. So

close. I just needed to get him inside. He yanked his wrist away from me and tried to back up a step. I moved around him, standing directly in front of his path to the exit. I stepped closer to him, and, still apparently repulsed by me, he was forced to take a step back. One step closer to the box.

I worked cautiously, moving closer step by step until I had cornered him against the container. He had no room left to back away. The backs of his legs pressed against the edge of the box. My arms shot out and I jabbed him in the chest, causing him to lose his balance and fall backward into the box. He hissed as he fell, and as his back hit the bottom of the container, he immediately gathered himself to spring out. But due to the surprise I'd given him, he was slower than me. Careful that neither of his hands was in the way of the lid, I brought the lid crashing down over his head.

Now the key. I need the key!

I gazed wildly around the room, relieved to spot a chain of keys on the floor. I fumbled for the right one and slid it into the lock, clicking the lid shut. Braithe beat the box's lid hard. But it didn't matter how strong he was. He wouldn't be able to get out of this box unless I opened it with the key. I'd learned that much from when I'd locked Benjamin in it. Benjamin was strong, stronger than most vampires. I'd been afraid that after he came to from the drug we had injected him with, he might be able to smash his way out of the box, even though he carried the essence of an Elder inside him. His inability to do so confirmed my belief about the box—its creator had caused its walls to be impervious to both subtle and physical beings.

I heaved out a huge sigh of relief and took a step back, eyeing the length of the box. Now I needed to get the box out of this room. Vomit was rising at the back of my throat from the amount of time I'd been forced to endure the werewolf's stench and from how wet and sticky my entire body felt from the vile fluid. I couldn't wait to get out of here and rinse myself off in the ocean.

But for now, I extended my claws and drove my fists though the exposed belly of the dead werewolf. There was another sickening squelch as I burst through bloated skin and more fluid sprayed onto my face. Biting my lips together so hard they almost bled, I pulled out two handfuls of the werewolf's decaying insides and smeared them over my body. As much as I wanted to cry in horror at what I was doing to myself, I was about to return to the deck where all the Bloodless would likely be—and I needed to make sure that I was topped up on stink.

Once I was satisfied that the new layer was thick enough,

I slid the key to the box off the keychain and slipped it safely into my bra. Then I left the room. The corridor outside was empty now. I climbed back up to the deck to see that the Bloodless had returned here. Before I looked up at the sky to search for Aisha, my eyes were drawn to the part of the deck where Arletta still lay, her transformation now more terrifying than ever. She was pulling out huge clumps of her long hair with one hand while the other ripped away the clothes from her body, rendering her emaciated form stark naked. Her breasts had flattened, and in fact all fat on her body had shriveled away. Her once rounded cheeks had closed in on themselves, and she now looked gaunt as a ghost.

I looked around for Colin and Frederick. I wanted to take them all with me to the witch's island, but it would look too suspicious to Aisha if I handpicked Frederick and Colin—especially because they bore a slight resemblance to Braithe, even in his wraithlike form. She might even guess that they had been my companions, or "accomplices" as she had referred to them. As it was, she was ignorant of the fact, and I had to try to keep it that way.

Now that I was above the deck, a crowd of Bloodless noticed me but, to my relief, shuffled further away from my reeking self.

"Hey," Aisha called down to me. I looked up to see the jinni hovering over me. "What happened to you?" She glared at me with disgust, wrinkling her nose. "Augh. What did you just take a bath in?"

"The fluids of a werewolf corpse," I replied darkly.

"Ohhh." A contented smile lit up Aisha's face. "I forgot about that little surprise. So did you manage it?"

"Yes," I grunted, uncertain how she knew about the werewolf—or heck, how she'd even escaped the box to begin with. "I managed to get one Bloodless into the box."

"Well, that is surprising," Aisha murmured. "I didn't expect you to make it out alive."

I looked at her sourly before returning my gaze to Arletta. *Maybe I could try to bring her with us at least...* I cleared my throat, still holding my nose to avoid the stench. "It occurred to me that we ought to bring a female too," I said, trying to make my voice sound casual.

Aisha furrowed her brows. Suspicion had already sparked in her eyes. "Why do you say that?" As her gaze shifted to Arletta, I saw that she'd already guessed the answer.

"I just thought—"

"You just thought nothing," she interrupted. She shook her head, her eyes narrowing on me. "I wasn't born yesterday. You simply want to bring your friend along."

"No," I protested, albeit unconvincingly. "We could take another female. It doesn't have to be Arletta." I should've just shut up. Aisha had already seen through me regarding Arletta, and by trying to save face, I was just digging a deeper hole for myself. I didn't want to have to go hunting after another one of these creatures—likely needing to cover myself with another few handfuls of maggot-ridden intestines in the process.

Thankfully, Aisha wasn't in the mood for waiting around longer. "No. You've caught one. He'll be enough of a specimen to take to the witch."

I decided that it was best not to press the matter, even as I looked back over at Arletta, now completely bald. She'd left her spot in the corner of the deck and had wandered over to the rest of them.

At least I'd managed to get Braithe. Aisha had no idea that he was one of my comrades. I didn't see how she would ever find out.

Now we could take him to the witch and perhaps, just perhaps I could strike a deal with her and persuade her to find a cure for him.

"So where's the box?" Aisha asked.

"I'll take you there," I said. Aisha thinned her body until she was in her subtle state—a state that allowed her to pass through solid walls. I led her back down through the trap door and along the corridor to the storage room where I'd left the box.

"God in heaven!" Aisha cried, coughing. "Ugh, that is so gross!"

I was in no mood to listen to her grumbling, as I stood here with practically every inch of me covered with bits of the corpse. I pointed to the box. "You should know it well enough by now," I muttered darkly.

"And whereabouts exactly is the exit that leads to the lifeboats?" Aisha asked. "There are a few strung up over the edge of the ship."

"Lifeboats?" I was taken aback by her question. "Why do we need lifeboats?" *Why can't she just use her magic to vanish us all away from here?*

"Just answer the question," Aisha snapped.

"Uh, okay. Follow me." I led her to the exit she requested. When I opened the door, it led out onto a small balcony, on either side of which were steps leading down toward hanging boats.

"All right," Aisha said coolly, eyeing the boat. "Now go bring the box here," she instructed me, with a nod of her head toward the door.

"Can't you do it by magic?" I asked, looking at her in

dismay. "It would be a lot faster."

She shot me another glare. "Just do it."

Blowing out in irritation, I gave in—what other option did I have?—and hurried back along the corridor. The soles of my feet were moist with blood and grime, and I almost slipped as I reached the storage room. Planting my hands on either side of the huge box, I gained as firm a grip as I could before dragging it out of the room, along the corridor and to the balcony where an impatient Aisha waited. Here, thankfully, she helped me lower the box onto one of the boats but strangely, she still didn't bother to use her magic. She resumed her physical form and manually helped me lift it. Although it confused me, I was too distracted to think much of it.

Once the box was in the center of the small boat, Aisha and I moved into it. Grabbing hold of the ropes that held the boat in place against the side of my ship, I lowered us down slowly into the waves. But now we needed an engine. Still holding onto the ropes that lined this side of the ship, I maneuvered us around it until we reached the bow where the sharks swam. I pulled us closer to the dangling reins and grabbed two of them, snatching them for ourselves. These two sharks would be more than powerful enough to give us good speed. The lifeboat being specifically designed for vampires, there was a small covering to give shelter from the sun. But I hoped that we would reach the witch doctor's island well before sunrise.

CHAPTER 8: RIVER

I was pulled unceremoniously from sleep by a lurch of the submarine. It came so suddenly, I almost rolled off the bed. I sat up slowly, opening my eyes and rubbing my face with my bound hands.

The residue of a dream still remained in my head. It'd been one of the most vivid dreams I'd ever had. It had started with a reunion of family and old friends. Even my father had been present, having been let out of jail early. He'd sat near my mother at the table and they had been talking and actually getting along. He swore that he'd given up his addiction, and was willing to undergo routine medical checks to prove it to us. He said that he'd already found a new job and he wanted to move back in with us. To care and provide for us. To be the father that he'd rarely ever been.

Then Ben had entered the room. Suddenly, I felt a weight around my ring finger and remembered... Ben and I were engaged. He had asked me some time ago—although the memory was foggy. My fiancé's entrance caused the dinner to become so much more than a family reunion. This meal would now also mark the announcement of Ben's and my engagement. Of course, I'd been keeping it a secret until now. I had wanted to keep it a surprise for when Ben returned from his long journey.

I could barely contain my excitement as he walked over to me, and I made room for him to take a seat. As I announced the news to my parents, family and friends, my heart swelled. I reveled in the look of happiness on their faces, the acceptance and approval in their eyes as they looked Ben over. It was almost as though they already knew him to be the right man for me, even though, other than my mother and siblings, nobody else in the room had ever met Ben before.

Then my younger sister asked me when the wedding was and... I blanked. Strangely, Ben and I had never discussed a wedding. And he looked... so uncomfortable when I glanced at him. Then he vanished completely, leaving me standing alone, my left hand still raised in midair to show my ring, but with no fiancé to introduce beside me.

Everyone else around the table looked confused, no doubt wondering why he had vanished or where he had gone. Perhaps they were even worrying on my behalf and pitying me. I found myself digging my ring finger back into the folds of my dress and pulling up a chair to sit back down. I cleared my throat and tried to steer the conversation to another subject. Tried to forget that Ben had ever appeared in the first place.

Then, toward the end of the meal, the ring itself vanished from my finger. And even the memory of his arrival began to fade, and it began to feel as though Ben's appearance had been nothing but a dream within a dream.

But why do I keep dreaming of Ben?

And where is he now?

It killed me that I didn't even know if he was still alive. I hadn't yet managed to find out from Derek and Sofia how their journey to the realm of the jinn had gone. Were the jinn still protecting him? *Is he still fleeing from the Elder?*

My anxiety over Ben was soon interrupted, however, as it felt like the submarine shuddered to a complete stop. Loud footsteps sounded all around me—above me, in the corridor outside, and also below me. It sounded like they were all heading in one direction. Then the lock of my door clicked open, and in stepped a hunter.

Not the tall, wiry man who'd come to see me before. This time, it was a woman—although she looked stronger and bulkier than most men I'd ever laid eyes on and she was incredibly tall. I would estimate six feet in height. If it hadn't been for the curve of her breasts and hips, she might've even been mistaken for a man. Her face was certainly gruff enough, and she had short hair that spiked upward in bristles. She wore a black top and pants just like the rest of the hunters, and she was carrying a gun in her hand, similar to the small silver one the man had entered with earlier.

She took my arm none too gently and pulled me off the bed. My feet being bound, I almost tripped as they hit the floor.

"I'm going to free your legs, all right?" she said, furrowing her bushy brows. "Though I warn you not to try anything."

She pressed the end of her gun against my stomach as she knelt down on the floor. Withdrawing a small key from her pocket with her other hand, she freed my feet. Only once the cuffs were released did I realize just how sore my ankles had become. The metal was rough and they hadn't left enough room between the restraints and my flesh. Red raw marks now marred my ankles, but I was grateful that at least I could walk normally again.

The hunter resumed her hold on my arm and led me out of the room. When we emerged in the corridor, I saw I'd been right in my observation that everybody was heading in the same direction. She led me past cabin after cabin until we reached a staircase. We hurried up it and emerged on the uppermost level of the submarine. A hatch was open in the roof, and a blinding light spilled down from it. Sunshine. Yet I didn't feel even the slightest bit of warmth. An icy draught leaked through the hatch, causing a painful chill to sweep through me.

Hunters were lining up to climb out of the exit, and my female escort was already putting us in the line. As we reached the stairs, she motioned for me to begin climbing up first. I felt the barrel of her gun against my back as I mounted the stairs. Poking my head out of the hatch, I was momentarily blinded by the brightness.

Surrounding the submarine was a rough sea, or was it an ocean? The vessel floated by an icy jetty, beyond which was a world of sprawling, virgin-white mountains. It was snowing now, even as I cast my eyes around, chilly flakes settling on my nose and cheeks. My body began to shiver more strongly.

"What are you waiting for?" the female hunter beneath

me called. "You're holding everyone up."

I couldn't bring myself to apologize. My fingers numb, I gripped the ice-cold metal railing and pulled myself onto the roof. The chill of the metal beneath the soles of my bare feet came like an electric shock.

I couldn't handle this. I was going to die of hypothermia. *What are these hunters thinking?* The female hunter emerged quickly after me, wearing a puffer jacket. She resumed her hold on my arm and pulled me down to the ground.

I yelped as my feet sank into what felt like four inches of snow.

"I can't do this," I breathed. "I'm going to die of cold." My wrists being bound together, I couldn't even wrap my arms around myself.

The hunter paused, then frowned. "Curious," she murmured. As her eyes trailed the crowd of hunters now trudging away from the submarine, I hoped that she was going to ask if anybody had some spare boots and a coat. Instead, she called out to a man at the front of the group. "Mark. Come take a look at this."

Mark, as he turned around to face us, was the same tall, lithe man who had drawn blood from me. Now his black uniform was cloaked in a long gray coat, his hands covered by black leather gloves. He wore a light gray scarf wrapped around his neck and a moleskin hat. He left the hunter he had been in the middle of a conversation with and filtered through the crowd toward us.

"She's cold," the female hunter said, still eyeing me with surprise.

You got that right. Now just hand me a coat.

"I am a half-blood," I said through gritted teeth, fighting to maintain a semblance of patience. "That means that I feel the cold more than a human. I need boots and a coat. Now."

Mark removed one of his gloves and brushed his fingers gently over my right hand, like he was gauging my temperature.

"Cold enough?" I asked bitterly, mimicking one of his short, fake smiles.

"And you have felt the cold like this since the day you were... half-turned?" he asked, ignoring my snide remark. He studied my face intensely.

I nodded vigorously. I could barely even talk now between my chattering teeth.

Still, he remained eyeing me until finally, he raised his gaze to the female hunter. "Beatrice, go fetch some spare clothes from the sub before Charlie locks it. You should find something suitable in the galley, by the coat hangers."

Beatrice obeyed Mark's command and returned to the

submarine. She returned quickly with a puffer jacket—similar to her own—and a pair of invitingly fluffy boots. She removed my handcuffs so that I could pull on both items. Although my bones would take a while to warm again, I heaved a sigh of relief.

"And is that better?" Mark asked, clearly out of biological curiosity rather than actual care for my comfort.

I nodded.

"Let's continue," Mark said.

Beatrice replaced the handcuffs and the three of us moved forward swiftly to catch up with the others. They all stopped and gathered in a spot about twenty feet ahead of us. As Beatrice, Mark and I neared, I caught sight of grey concrete and realized that we'd arrived at a helipad.

My ears soon picked up on the sound of a helicopter slicing through the air above us. A large black chopper was approaching. Touching down on the strip, it caused a mini-snowstorm. The door to the aircraft opened, and a ramp descended. Hunters began hurrying into the chopper. Beatrice, Mark and I were the last to enter. The aircraft looked even bigger from the inside, almost the size of a commercial airplane. One of the rows nearest to the front was empty, containing five seats in total.

Beatrice pushed me down in the window seat while she

sat next to me. Gazing out at the frosty landscape, I wondered where in the world we were. Somewhere in the United States? Canada? I wasn't sure if we had been traveling long enough to have ventured to somewhere in Europe.

Beatrice removed restraints from her puffy coat and bent down to my ankles. She was about to bind me again when Mark stopped her.

"I don't think there's a need for that," he said, as he settled in his own seat next to Beatrice. I couldn't miss the bulge in the pocket of his coat—no doubt a gun. "I suspect she won't try anything foolish."

She. It occurred to me that not one of them had even asked what my name was yet.

I gazed around at the other hunters in the packed aircraft. It certainly would be insane to try anything now. I slumped back in my chair, resuming my focus out of the window. I was glad that I'd gotten the window seat. Though, as the chopper launched into the air, I wasn't exactly able to gain any better idea as to where we were. All I got was confirmation that I was in the middle of an icy nowhere.

I kept hoping that I would spy a small village, or maybe even a town tucked away somewhere in the mountains. But there was no sign of human settlement… until, hours into the flight, the helicopter tilted in a change of direction, and

I caught sight of a scattering of buildings perched among the peaks. They were all identical in size and design. Rectangular buildings, their exteriors appeared to be constructed out of tinted glass—glass that glaringly reflected the harsh sunshine. They were perhaps ten stories in height. Then I spotted a helipad—much larger than the one near the jetty. Dozens of helicopters were parked around it, all of them large and black like the one we were traveling in. A little further along from the strip was a parking lot, jam-packed with shiny SUVs.

"Would you tell me where we are?" I asked Beatrice, irritably.

To my annoyance, she acted as though she hadn't heard me. I looked along to the next seat where Mark sat. He'd donned a pair of headphones.

Beyond frustrated, I twisted in my seat to face the rest of the aircraft behind me. I cleared my throat and asked loudly, "Would someone be so *kind* as to tell me where we are?"

I had irritated Beatrice enough for her to stop ignoring me. "It doesn't matter where we are," she answered gruffly. "It doesn't make any difference to you. You'll be kept with us as long as you're needed." She grabbed my arm and tugged on me to face forward again.

"How long will that be?" I asked, my hopes lifting a little.

Beatrice's phrasing indicated that perhaps there would come a time when they were actually finished with me. Hopefully they would let me go and not kill me.

Mark replied this time, having removed his headphones at the commotion I was causing. His eyes dug into me. "As I told you before, the more you cooperate with us, the better it will be for you."

He and Beatrice fell silent after that, and so did I. I didn't think it wise to annoy these hunters too much, considering that any one of them could pull out a gun and shoot me at any moment.

I pursed my lips and glanced out of the window again, watching the buildings as the helicopter positioned itself above the landing strip and began descending. It landed on the concrete with a shudder and the hunters immediately rose to their feet. The door opened, and everyone began piling out, keeping their heads low beneath the rotors. I didn't wait for Beatrice to grab my arm. I stood up and followed the crowd obediently, she and Mark close behind me.

Climbing down the ramp, I was once again assaulted by the cold. Though, thankfully not for long. Mark and Beatrice led me straight into one of the glass buildings. I gazed around as we stepped into what appeared to be a reception area. Aside from a long desk in one corner where four women sat—I wasn't surprised to see them also dressed in black—the furnishings were minimal. The floors were made of a kind of white granite that resembled the blanket of snow outside. It was like the reception area of an exceptionally swanky business center, although the starkness of the place gave it a clinical feel, more like an exclusive private hospital.

"You can head off now, Beatrice," Mark said. "I'll handle things from here."

She nodded and, eyeing me briefly once more, took off toward a line of elevators on the opposite side of the room.

Mark led me to the reception desk.

"I need a room in the east wing," he said to one of the receptionists.

She eyed me briefly before consulting a computer. "56A is unoccupied," she replied.

"That'll do fine," Mark said.

The woman walked to a cabinet and withdrew a key. She handed it to Mark, who then led me toward the elevators. By now all of the other hunters had cleared off, and as the elevator arrived and we stepped inside, I was left standing awkwardly, alone with this stranger.

He pushed the button for the third floor. On arrival, the

doors dinged open and we emerged in a wide corridor which was mostly empty except for the odd hunter moving in and out of rooms. There was a line of large, beechwood doors to our right, while to our left was nothing but glass, granting us a view out onto the snowy terrain. My stomach was too tense for me to admire how beautiful it was.

We reached the end of the corridor and arrived at the entrance of a glass tunnel. It was a walkway, connecting this building to the neighboring one on the opposite mountain peak. It reminded me a little of the glass walkways that connected some of the treehouses in the Residences back in The Shade. As we moved through the transparent tunnel, to my discomfort, the floor was also made of glass—allowing a more than generous view of the steep drop below.

I began to lose track of where he was taking me after that. We wound around more corridors, stepped into more elevators, and passed along more transparent walkways from one building to another.

All the while, I wished that Mark would stop being so tight-lipped and just put me out of my misery. He already knew that I was helpless. Just knowing my location wouldn't make it any easier for me to escape. I was certain that they'd already searched me thoroughly for any kind of communication device. I had no way of communicating with the outside world.

Eventually, as I'd just about had enough of all the walking, we arrived inside a huge enclosed courtyard. Its dome ceiling was—no surprise—made of glass, allowing sunshine to stream through and illuminate the place. As he began leading me along one of the wide verandas, I found myself peering through full-glass doors into… prison cells? To my shock, they appeared to be filled with supernaturals— grotesque birdlike creatures that resembled harpies I'd read about in fairytales, ogres in some of the larger cells, and other strange creatures that I wasn't yet knowledgeable enough to even put a name to. He kept walking, leading me deeper into the courtyard until I spotted a large tank of water filled with merfolk. There must have been at least thirty in there, men and women alike.

Where did they get them all from? Perhaps that was a dumb question. I guessed that the supernaturals must have ventured into the human realm and gotten themselves caught. Strangely, I couldn't spot a single vampire. The fact that the hunters had been intending to kill Derek, Sofia and Aiden on that cluster of rocks, coupled with the lack of vampires here, made me think that perhaps the hunters weren't that interested in them anymore. Perhaps the hunters had learnt all they wished to know over the years, and now simply saw vampires as a pest to be exterminated.

Mark led me closer to the tank of merfolk. Their unpleasant faces were livid as we approached, and they began pounding their fists against the glass container so violently I feared they'd smash it. I could only wonder how the hunters had managed to make the glass so strong as to withstand the strength of all these supernaturals. Finally, Mark stopped outside a glass door, directly opposite to the merfolk tank. He opened it with a key and pushed it wide open for me to step inside.

"This will be your room while you're here," he said, entering after me and glancing briefly around the room.

While you're here. Again, his choice of words gave me hope that perhaps there was light at the end of the tunnel. I just wished that I knew how long this tunnel was.

To my surprise, Mark reached for my wrists and freed me of the restraints. Then he swept across the room and out of the door, locking it behind him. I listened to the sound of his resounding footsteps disappearing down the veranda.

I gazed around the empty room. There were lots of things I could fault the hunters for, but cleanliness certainly wasn't one of them. If anything, this room appeared to be even cleaner than the cabin they'd given me in the submarine. The bed also had a softer, deeper mattress and two perky pillows.

The floor was sparkling clean, cleaner than many a restaurant plate I'd eaten from in the past. Rubbing my sore wrists together, I checked out the basic bathroom furnishings before taking a seat on the bed, testing its softness. There was a small bedside table with a lamp, and what appeared to be a fresh set of clothes—plain black clothes, a top and pants— just like those the hunters wore.

Heaving a deep sigh, I shuffled backward on the mattress until my back hit the wall. I wrapped myself in the wool blanket. Although the temperature was moderate in this room, I was still recovering from the cold outside. At least I felt a little less tense now that I was on my own again. For the first time, I realized that I was starving. My stomach ached. I had to hope they'd give me something to eat later.

I leaned my head against the wall and stared out of the glass door at the tank of merfolk, perfectly positioned for me to have full view of. To my discomfort, they were all glaring at me. There weren't even curtains or a blind I could pull across the door for some privacy.

Their grotesque features twisted as they made faces at me, as though I was the one responsible for imprisoning them in the tank.

Great, I grumbled to myself. *Just the creatures I wanted to be staring at all day.*

CHAPTER 9: BEN

I'd followed River off the submarine, stayed close to her in the helicopter, and then accompanied her and Mark to her new room in the hunters' lair. Throughout the journey, I'd been paying close attention to anything that could possibly give me an idea of where we were. I'd even found myself looking for license plates in case any of them gave me a clue. Frustratingly, none of the vehicles possessed them. Either they were new vehicles still awaiting plates or the hunters had some special pass from the government that didn't require them to obey laws like everyone else.

I imagined that the impressive facility had also been funded by the government. It all looked brand new—I doubted it had been standing for long. It didn't take long for me to figure out this was some kind of research center, and this suspicion was only verified once we entered the courtyard filled with a myriad of supernatural creatures.

Now that River was locked in her room, it was time that I left her to have a look around. I guessed that nobody would bother her again for at least an hour, since many of the hunters had just arrived back from a long journey and would probably be busy settling back into their own quarters.

Moving closer to her bed as she leaned against the wall, I couldn't help but move my lips over her forehead before I left the cell.

I'd tried to pay attention to my surroundings on the way to the courtyard, but this place was winding like a maze. I might get lost if I wasn't careful. And it wasn't like I could stop and ask someone for directions. To start with, I remained in the same building as the courtyard, although as it turned out, there wasn't much else of interest here. Mostly I found large, empty meeting-type rooms with long tables and projectors, and on some of the lower levels, there were what appeared to be hunters' residential quarters. There were hunters around, but I didn't find any conversations of relevance to eavesdrop on.

Before passing through to the next building, I decided to

explore outside. Something told me that with my unearthly speed, it might be faster than continuing my attempts to eavesdrop. During the flight, I'd been looking out of the helicopter alongside River, hoping to see a nearby town. I hadn't spotted any, but the windows had been small and provided only limited vision. With hindsight, I should've stuck my head right through the wall of the aircraft.

I left the building where River was being kept and headed to the parking lot. Passing the many vehicles, I was most interested in the road that branched off in the far corner of the lot. It wound right through the mountain range. If anything would lead to a town or village, surely this road would.

And so I followed it, racing as fast as I could. It led me through the sprawling mountains, sometimes rising, sometimes descending, and I was beginning to grow impatient to see where it led. I felt nervous about how much time was passing. I had no way of telling the time, but I guessed it had been fifteen minutes. I had already managed to travel so many miles, I'd lost all sight of the hunters' base up near the peaks. Still, I could see no signs of civilization. Just an endless blanket of snow.

After half an hour, I even considered turning back and returning to my original plan of eavesdropping until I found out the location. I didn't have time to burn. I didn't know for sure if the hunters were telling the truth that they didn't want to kill River, and I wasn't willing to take the risk. I needed to urgently get help from The Shade.

I was on the verge of turning around and heading back to the hunters' lair when the universe finally threw me a bone. Looming on the horizon was another road. A much larger road than the one I'd been following. I even spotted a couple of cars trundling along, their metal exteriors glinting in the sunshine. The landscape was also beginning to flatten.

I hurried forward until I reached the road. I looked left and right for a sign post, but saw none. What I did spot, however, about two miles to my right down this highway, was what appeared to be a grand hotel… and as I approached nearer, I realized that it was a ski resort.

"Bluesky Peaks Resort," read the sign nailed across the large building, complete with the symbol of a pair of skis. A large American flag flowed in the breeze, erected directly in front of the resort. I guessed that meant we were still in the United States. Some comfort at least. I'd feared that we might have traveled further.

Now, I just needed to remember the name of the resort. It wouldn't be difficult for whoever I found in The Shade to locate it. A simple internet search should bring up the exact location of the place. In fact, as I looked more closely, I noticed a website address nailed in smaller letters just beneath the main sign. Being situated right next to this main highway, it was also close to the road that wound through the mountains to the hunters' lair. I hadn't noticed any other roads branching off from that track, so the journey from here should be fairly straightforward.

I committed the name of the resort into my memory, along with the website, and then I didn't have another moment to lose. I returned to the winding road and followed it all the way back to the hunters' parking lot.

I needed to turn my thoughts to how the heck I was going to make it back to The Shade in any reasonable amount of time. Jeramiah wasn't there to play the Pied Piper for me anymore.

But first I wanted to check on River one last time. I had no way of knowing exactly how long I'd be gone, and although I would be even more powerless to help her hundreds of miles away, I needed to see that she was okay before I left. I hurried back to the courtyard and arrived outside her door. But when I peered inside, she was gone.

CHAPTER 10: RIVER

I was beginning to feel bored out of my mind. The hunters might have kept the cells clean and decent, but the lack of anything to do in them was torturous. What did they expect their prisoners to do all day? Nothing, I guessed.

I would've killed for a book to read. Or anything to help take my mind off time passing… and the crude gestures the merfolk had started making to me from their tank. I guessed that they were just as bored as I was. I glared daggers back at them for lack of anything else to do. In the end, I retreated to the bathroom and stepped in the shower, pleased that the water was hot. I found the shower comforting, and I would've stayed there for a lot longer if I hadn't heard keys being inserted into my cell door. As it clicked open, I leapt from the shower and grabbed a towel, wrapping it tightly around me. I opened the door just a fraction to see who it was.

My eyes were met by Mark's icy blue ones. I quickly shut the door again.

"What do you want?" I called. Truth be told, I had expected him to return sooner.

"I'd like you to come with me."

I shouldn't have expected anything less cryptic from him by now.

"Okay," I muttered. "Let me get dressed."

I fumbled around in the bathroom, looking for my clothes before realizing that I had left them on the bed outside. *Dammit.*

"Uh, would you hand me my clothes?" I called to Mark through the door. "They should be on the mattress."

I opened the door again, just wide enough to thrust out my hand. A few seconds later, he had planted my clothes into my palm and I pulled them in through the door before closing it again behind me. I hurriedly dried myself and got dressed. Glancing in the mirror, I realized for the first time how wrecked I looked. I had dark shadows under my eyes and in general looked like I hadn't had a wink of sleep in days. I gathered my hair above my head and wrapped it in a tight bun before leaving the bathroom.

Reentering the main room, I took in Mark's appearance properly. He was wearing a change of clothes, and whereas he'd had a shadow of stubble around his sharp jawline before, now it was shaved clean. His black hair was combed back neatly, and he smelled of minty aftershave.

He wasn't holding a gun this time, although I was sure that he was armed with one—perhaps attached to the back of his belt.

I frowned at him. "Where do you want to take me?"

"To our lab," he replied, eyeing me steadily.

Lab. Recalling his assurance that the more I cooperated, the better off I'd be, I moved to the door and stepped outside.

I wanted to ask what exactly they wanted me in the lab for, but I was fed up of asking questions only to be brushed off with non-answers. I guessed I'd find out soon enough what they wanted from me. Maybe even too soon for comfort.

Even now, Mark didn't bother to bind my wrists. It showed how small a threat the hunters had come to see me as, though I supposed that this could only work in my favor.

He gestured toward the exit of the courtyard and

indicated that I follow as he began heading toward it. We entered an elevator and embarked on a journey out of this building, along countless corridors and half a dozen glass walkways, until we arrived outside tall, stark white double doors on the ground floor of a building about a mile away from the one that held the courtyard. Mark flattened his thumb against a screen fixed near the handles. The device beeped, and the doors drew open as gracefully as curtains.

I stepped into a vast laboratory. The length of the tables that lined the stark white walls and the amount of sleek, state-of-the-art equipment they had in here was breathtaking.

"This is just the ground floor," Mark commented as he led me deeper into the room. Perhaps he'd noticed the awed expression on my face.

Mark stopped us in the center of the lab and pulled out a phone from his pocket. He dialed a number, his eyes falling on me as he waited for whomever he was calling to pick up.

"Jocelyn, I'm on the ground level." He spoke into the receiver. "We're waiting for you."

He hung up.

We stood for a few moments surrounded by the eerie silence of the lab before the sound of footsteps descending a staircase came from the far corner of the room. The set of doors swung open near a table of burners and out stepped a short, mousy woman with wide-rimmed spectacles and a tiny frame. Donning a dark blue lab coat, she hurried as she spotted us, the short heels of her shoes clacking against the sleek white floors.

Arriving next to us, she exchanged a knowing glance with Mark before reaching out to take my hand. I hesitated, glancing at Mark.

He nodded encouragingly. "Go with Jocelyn. She'll return you to your room once you're done."

Once I'm done with what?

I looked at this new Jocelyn woman untrustingly, but allowed her to lead me away all the same. I cast one more glance over my shoulder toward Mark as he left the room before the woman led me up a staircase. We climbed a single flight and arrived on the first floor—just as large and impressive as the one beneath. She led me across it toward a long, heavy black curtain that was sectioning off a portion of the lab. She parted the curtain and led me through it. I found myself staring at a row of treatment beds with more alien equipment crowded around them. She indicated a bed in front of it and nodded, smiling faintly.

"Make yourself comfortable," she said.

I doubted I could make myself comfortable in this lab

even if she presented me with a king-sized bed to stretch out on, but I did my best to acquiesce. She perched herself on a stool next to the bed and planted her foot down on a red button, which made the bed tilt upward slightly, until my back was at a forty-five degree angle.

Then she switched on a bright fluorescent lamp that hung directly over my face, apparently designed to blind a person. I was forced to close my eyes, bright spots swirling in the backs of my eyelids.

I couldn't see much of what she was doing after that, but I felt her probing my body with cool metal objects. She planted what felt like a stethoscope against my chest, then I felt bands around my upper arm which tensed and squeezed—apparently taking my blood pressure. An unpleasant rounded object covered with some kind of ice-cold gel roamed my neck, and it seemed to be giving off some kind of micro-electric current, as I felt an unpleasant stinging in my skin. Then, without asking for my permission, she rolled up the bottom of my shirt, revealing my bare lower abdomen. Using the same freezing cold gel-coated instrument, she ran it over my stomach, causing shivers to run through my body. I bit my lip, tensing.

"*What* are you doing?" I grunted.

"Just a few tests," she said lightly. "Nothing to worry

about."

It grated at my nerves the way she talked to me like I was a child. I couldn't help but wonder if she had a gun near her as she sat examining me. Though even if she didn't, and I managed to overpower her and escape, where would I go? Heck, I didn't even know that I could leave this laboratory. It had required Mark's thumbprint to enter, and it might not be possible even to exit this place without another authorized fingerprint. I guessed that I could try to drag Jocelyn along to the door and force her finger against the device… but then what? I was still in the middle of nowhere. I would likely freeze before I ever found help, or more likely, they would catch me first. I pushed away the fantasy of escape. If they didn't let me go voluntarily soon, I would have no choice but to attempt it… but when I did, I needed to have a good plan. Otherwise I would only find myself in worse trouble.

My focus returned to Jocelyn. She had finished freezing my stomach with her probe, and had hopefully put the damn thing away. She had now moved to my feet where, for reasons I couldn't fathom, she had begun digging her fingers against pressure points in my soles. I wanted to squirm away from her. I was ticklish down there.

"So, Jocelyn," I said, trying to avert my attention from the way she was touching me. Still, I kept my eyes closed to shield myself from the blinding light. "What do you do exactly?"

"I'm a scientist," she replied, "and a doctor. Depends on which day of the week it is, really."

"A scientist and a doctor of what?"

My question was met with silence.

I blew out a sigh. Why was I even still bothering to attempt to get some serious answers out of these people? They were all as tight-lipped as each other.

Neither of us spoke for what felt like the next ten minutes. Then, to my surprise, her stool scraped and she switched off the horrid lamp.

I opened my eyes to see her standing by my head and looking me over with a gleam of contentment in her eyes. She clutched a pad of paper in one hand which was filled with scribbled notes, though she was holding it at such an angle that I couldn't read them—no doubt a conscious move on her part.

"How old were you when you were half-turned?" she asked.

I felt bemused that still, nobody had bothered to ask my name.

"Seventeen," I replied.

An unnerving smile formed on her thin lips, the

satisfaction in her expression intensifying. "So young," she said. "Good."

Although curiosity burned inside me, I didn't even bother to ask her why that was good.

She placed her notepad on a nearby table and settled her pen on top of it. "Right," she said, straightening and rubbing her hands together. "We're almost done. I need you to do just one last thing for me, all right?"

No, it's not all right, but, of course, that was a rhetorical question, wasn't it?

She reached into a drawer and pulled out a thin plastic tube. "Go to the bathroom and fill this with your urine."

My lip curled. "I don't need to pee."

"No problem," she said briskly, even as she planted the tube into my right hand. "We can fix that." She moved over to a sink and, filling up a glass with water, returned and handed it to me. "Drink up."

I raised the glass gingerly to my lips and began to drink. I was actually thirsty, so I didn't object to topping up on water but... I hated being asked to fill up a tube of urine for anyone—even my doctor back home in New York—much less for these despicable hunters. Still, I had no choice.

I swallowed down three cupfuls until I felt the need to go. I spent as little time in the bathroom as possible doing the deed, and then returned to Jocelyn.

"Perfect!" she exclaimed, eyeing the tube of pee like it was liquid gold. "All right. I'll escort you back to your room."

She stowed my urine sample away in a drawer before leading me out of the lab. I was right in assuming that the place was locked from the inside too—Jocelyn had to plant her thumbprint onto a screen.

As we wound our way back to the courtyard, I muttered without even bothering to hide the irritation in my voice, "So are you satisfied with whatever tests you were doing?"

I'd said it out of annoyance rather than actually expecting a reply, but this time, she did choose to respond.

"Oh, more than satisfied," she said, that unnerving smile of hers returning to her lips.

I cocked my head to one side, raising a brow, as if daring her to continue.

She cleared her throat, excitement gleaming in her irises. "Let's just say… we were rather stupid to try to shoot you before."

Chapter 11: Ben

I tried to keep calm. River being absent from her cell didn't necessarily mean that something bad had happened to her. It could simply be that the hunters had wanted to examine her.

Still, I couldn't shake my nerves as I hurried out of the courtyard and went in search of her. I didn't know where to start looking. She could be in any one of these buildings, and the longer I spent looking for her, the more time it was going to take for me to get someone here who could help her. Searching for her was in this sense stupid, but I found it hard to fight my protective instinct and not at least verify her location before I left. The many hours I'd have to spend journeying back would be all the more torturous if I didn't.

Thankfully, I didn't have to search for too long. Several corridors along from the courtyard, I spotted her walking with a woman in a lab coat. River looked okay on a cursory glance, even if rather flustered and frustrated. They walked past me, and as they wound around a few corners, I followed them back inside the courtyard until they reached River's cell.

"I'm feeling hungry," River said to the woman before she left her alone in the room. "I don't need blood, I just eat regular human food. Could you get me something? And a bottle of water would be good, too."

The woman gave her a brief nod. "I'll arrange for something."

With that, the woman clicked River's door shut and turned on her heel, disappearing out of sight along the veranda.

River blew out a breath and plopped herself down on the bed. Her hands resting over her lower stomach, she stared blankly up at the ceiling. I wondered where the hunters had just taken her and what they had done to her.

But now I had to leave. Reluctantly, I tore my eyes away from River and swept out of the cell. As I emerged in the center of the courtyard, I didn't take a right turn toward the exit, like a normal person would. Instead, I drifted off the floor and headed upward, toward the glass ceiling. My body passed through it and out into the icy world beyond. Snow had begun to fall heavily, and the sky had clouded over.

Scanning my surroundings, I tried to gain a sense of direction and remember which way the ocean was. It couldn't have been all that far away, based on the length of the helicopter journey. I rose in the sky until I was high enough to see the mass of water far in the distance. If I had any luck, that would be the Pacific Ocean.

I was about to begin hurtling toward it at full speed when something directly beneath me caught my eye. A shiny black Hummer was trundling up the slope toward the parking lot. Since I'd arrived in this place, this was the first car that I'd spotted in motion. Despite my urgency to get a move on, I drifted down from the sky, closer to the vehicle.

It wasn't so much the SUV itself that interested me, but rather the container that was trailing along behind it. It looked like a rectangular box and was covered by a large beige canvas wrapping. It could've just been food supplies, or new equipment... but then two men wearing heavy coats and black boots stepped out of the vehicle and walked to the container. They knelt down beside the trailer and released the hooks that were holding the canvas in place.

With one strong tug, the two men hauled off the covering

to reveal... *What is that?*

The rectangular container turned out to be a cage, and within the cage was a creature that made my jaw fall open.

It was a small creature, about the size of a pony. Its smooth back was coated with golden brown fur, as was its long winding tail, and hind legs. They looked like those of a lion. While its head and front legs—which were in fact talons—belonged to some kind of carnivorous bird. And now I glimpsed wings—heavy, feathered wings, that appeared to have been bound together against its back to prevent it from flying.

As strange as it looked, I realized that I recognized this beast... It had all the features of a griffin— a supernatural creature that I'd never seen before in the flesh, and had only read about in books.

So griffins really do exist.

But how did the hunters find one? And what are they doing with it?

The griffin clacked its razor sharp beak and let out a loud screech—extraordinarily loud for its size. One of the men hurried back to the truck and, opening the back door, pulled out a blow gun. There was a sharp needle at the tip of it, and when the hunter aimed the weapon through the bars, the needle shot out and wedged itself into the creature's neck.

The griffin cawed again, by the sounds of it more out of anger than pain. Its legs staggered and gave way.

One of the men climbed onto the cage and reached its roof. He bent down and opened a hatch before sliding himself down inside the bars. He grabbed what looked like a sturdy, leather muzzle from a hook within the cage and fastened it firmly around the creature's hooked beak. Then the hunter who'd remained on the outside pressed a green button at the side of the cage, causing its back wall to shudder and lift open. The second man joined the first within the cage. They grabbed the griffin by a thick collar that was bound around its throat and tugged it out into the snow.

By now, the beast had become too weakened by whatever drug the hunter had shot at it to fight back, and even its shrieking had become more subdued. Still, it remained conscious enough to plant one foot in front of the other as the two hunters dragged it to the nearest building.

I ought to be in a desperate hurry to leave this place and reach the ocean, but as the hunters pulled that creature through the revolving glass doors, I simply couldn't hold myself back. I promised myself that I would stay here no longer than five more minutes just to see where they were taking that griffin, and followed them into the building.

As they emerged in an empty entrance area, one of the hunters hurried off into a room at the other end of the hall. He returned less than a minute later pushing a large trolley that resembled the type you'd find at airports, except wider. The hunter parked the trolley in front of the creature before the two of them worked together to usher the beast onto it. It was too sluggish to put up a fight. It just stepped onto it, almost obediently, before its legs folded beneath it and it sat down.

Then the men continued across the room, heading toward a corridor at the other side of it. One of them pushed the trolley, while the other pulled out a phone from his coat pocket. He dialed a number.

"We're back," he said after a moment. "We'll be in Room 98."

He returned the phone to his pocket and the two of them continued winding along the corridor with the griffin until they reached a set of double doors, just before the entrance of a glass walkway.

The man who wasn't pushing the trolley stamped his thumb against a screen, and the two doors slid open. They entered with the creature and stopped at the head of a long meeting table that ran down the center of the room. This looked like a boardroom similar to others that I'd passed through in the building where River was kept, except for one key difference. The walls of the other rooms had been mostly bare. But standing in this room, it was hard to spot even an inch of wall that wasn't covered with sketches. Weird sketches that looked like they belonged in a fantasy art studio. All of them depicted what looked like grotesque hybrids, combinations of apparently some kind of Earth animal and at least one body part of a supernatural creature. The limbs of a bear with the face of a werewolf. The body of a tiger with the distinctive black talons of a Hawk. Gruesome mutations that I could not have concocted in my wildest dreams. Even thoughts of River got pushed to the back of my mind as I gaped around the room at the pictures.

The double doors drew open again. I turned to see a tall, slim man entering. It was Mark. Holding a phone in his right hand, he approached the trolley and gazed down at the griffin. He bent down—fearlessly close to it—and tugged at the creature's neck, apparently allowing himself to get a better look at its face.

He stared at the griffin for several moments before nodding curtly and rising to his feet. He eyed the other two hunters. "Have you informed Evelyn yet?" he asked.

"Not yet," one of the men replied. "I thought you might want to do that."

Mark cleared his throat and punched a number into his phone. He raised it to his ear, but nobody picked up. "Her phone's switched off," he muttered. "I'll go find her. In the meantime, wait here."

"Yes, sir," the men murmured.

With that, Mark marched out of the room.

Although I knew that five minutes had already passed, I was beyond tempted to follow him and find out who this Evelyn person was, and what on earth these hunters were playing at. But I forced myself to my senses. *I don't have time.* Staying longer and trying to discover what they were doing would not help River. Not even if I managed to unravel everything about their activities. At least, not until I had someone from The Shade by my side.

I cast one last glance at the griffin before forcing myself to leave the room, although I was sure the scene I had just witnessed would haunt me long after I had left the facility.

Chapter 12: River

That night, as I drifted off to sleep, I hoped that I would dream of Ben again. As disturbing as the previous dreams involving him had been... I missed him so much. I missed him more than I'd ever thought it possible to miss a person. I felt hollow thinking back over the weeks and months we'd spent together before getting separated. *What I wouldn't give to see him again...*

But that night, he didn't make an appearance in my subconscious. Instead, my sleep was hijacked by a nightmare. My experience from the previous day, being probed and examined by Jocelyn in the lab, morphed into an inescapable horror movie, starring me as the hapless victim. She and a crowd of other doctor-scientists in lab coats were gathered round me on an operating table, freely helping themselves to pieces of my body and stuffing them in plastic tubes like the one I'd filled with urine. They had not even bothered to give me a general anesthetic. I was conscious of every cut, every nip, every pull of my flesh…

I woke with a start, sitting bolt upright in bed. I found myself sweating and panting heavily. I swallowed hard, running my hands over my face.

It was just a dream. Just a dream. Granted, those words didn't have the same effect on me that they would've done a week ago—before the inexplicably prophetic dream involving Ben predicting Jeramiah's kidnapping of Ben's parents and grandfather.

I glanced at the small digital clock on my bedside table. 3:07 AM.

Although the temperature in my cell was mild, I started to shiver. I was feeling cold again. Too cold. Nothing new, of course. Unbearable chills could creep into my bones even in the middle of a desert. Even after all the time I'd had to get used to the body of a half-blood, I still hadn't been able to figure out a pattern for my coldness. There didn't seem to be any rhyme or reason for when the shivering came on—it just did, and all I could do was wrap myself up.

But even the blanket and the puffer jacket Beatrice had given me weren't enough to provide sufficient warmth. I slid out of bed and entered the bathroom, where I ran myself a hot bath. Thankfully, this was effective. I continued topping up the tub with hot water every few minutes until the pain in my joints ebbed away to a more manageable level. I must have been soaking for about an hour before hoisting myself out and drying off. I changed into the same clothes I'd worn yesterday, since I hadn't yet been provided with fresh ones.

I froze as the main door to my room clicked.

Stepping out, I almost yelped as I found myself face to face with a woman, standing right in the center of my dark room. My heart leapt in my throat. It took a few seconds for me to register that it was a familiar face. Jocelyn. Why hadn't she turned on the light? She looked so creepy standing there so still, her arrival so unexpected. And at this time in the morning? I checked the clock. 4:13 AM.

"What are you doing here?" I asked, half tense as I noticed the large black bag she was carrying on her back, and half irritated that she would intrude on my privacy at this unholy hour.

"You informed me that you were hungry."

I stared at her in disbelief. "Uh, yes. *Dinner* would have been nice." Just thinking about food made my stomach whine. "I didn't expect you to come disturbing me at four in the morning."

"Well, I'm sorry for the delay, but I've brought you some food."

I moved over to the light switch and flicked it on, removing the creepy shadows that had been playing across her face. This short, mousy-haired woman looked much less threatening beneath the light.

She removed the bag from her back and lowered it to the floor. I took a seat on the bed and watched as she pulled out three aluminum foil-wrapped packages. She laid them all out on my bedside table, along with two bottles of water.

"Thank you," I murmured, eyeing the food and wondering what it was exactly. I reached out and touched the nearest package to me—it was soft and, to my pleasant surprise, it was also warm.

I glanced back at Jocelyn. Her bag still remained where she'd placed it on the floor, and she'd made not even the slightest show of leaving the room. She just stood at the end of my bed, watching me.

"Thank you," I said again, louder this time, discarding all subtleties. "I am sure that this food is just fine."

She smiled tersely. "Good. Then why don't you eat? You haven't lost your appetite, have you?"

I frowned at her, the warm food suddenly seeming less appealing. I didn't fancy eating with this woman watching me like I was some kind of zoo animal.

"I would rather eat alone," I said, eyeing her pointedly.

She nodded, though she still made no motion to move.

"I want you to leave."

Again, she just nodded, blankly, even as she remained glued to her spot.

I gave up at this point. She was obviously going to stay in my room and watch me whether I liked it or not. I twisted on the bed and turned my focus on the food. I picked up the largest package first—the warm one. I unwrapped the foil to reveal a whole grain baguette. I parted it, examining the filling. It was stuffed with tomatoes, cheese, avocado and some kind of pungent mustard. I took my first bite, surprised that it tasted a lot better than it smelt.

Ignoring Jocelyn as best as I could, I finished the whole baguette in a matter of minutes and then moved on to the next item. An apple. I wolfed that down, leaving me with the final package—a tub of rice pudding. After eating that, I tossed the foil in the trash before swigging down some water and leaning back in bed.

"Satisfied?" Jocelyn asked, breaking the silence.

I nodded stiffly before sinking down into the mattress and

pulling the blanket over me. I was beginning to feel sleepy again. It had taken me a long time to drift off last night and, thanks to the nightmare, I had not been sleeping long at all. Then the hot bath, combined with the meal, made me want to doze off again.

Jocelyn still didn't take the hint to leave, not even after I turned out the light and buried my head in my pillow.

I sensed her drawing closer. "What was your name?" she asked.

I rolled over in bed to glare up at her. I wondered what made her suddenly curious to know my name.

"Alice," I grumbled, for why should I tell the truth? Ben had used a false name when in hostile territory, and I didn't see why I shouldn't do the same.

"Okay, Alice. You need to come with me now."

My face deadpanned. "Are you kidding me?"

She shook her head. "Come." She held out her hand for me to take.

Although I was beginning to feel half-asleep, I didn't know what else I could do than obey. I swung my legs off the bed, and stood up.

"Where do you wanna take me now?"

"Back to the lab."

To go create some fresh material for my nightmares. Great. I gritted my teeth.

She picked up the backpack from the floor and stepped outside the room. As she led me toward the exit of the courtyard, I glanced at the merfolk in the tank—even they appeared to be still sleeping at this early hour. We left the prison area and she led me back to the laboratory. She pressed her thumb against the screen next to the doors to open them. When we stepped inside, the ground floor of the lab was dark, except for shafts of moonlight trickling eerily through the glass walls at the far end of the room.

Jocelyn's small heeled shoes clacked against the sleek floor as she moved further inside and reached for a light switch. The lights flickered on, their stark fluorescence momentarily blinding me. As she led me toward the staircase, I expected her to stop at the same level as she had the last time—perhaps even take me to the same treatment table she'd been examining me on before. But she didn't. She kept leading me higher until we reached the fourth floor. My throat was dry as she strayed from the staircase and entered through a glass door, emerging in a section of the lab that was entirely new to me. The center of the large rectangular room was filled with tables, like the other floors I'd seen so far, but the walls were steel and lined with doors—one of which Jocelyn began moving toward. She opened the door on the other side of the room and gestured for me to enter after her.

I froze as soon as I laid eyes on the contents of the room. From the sturdiness of the table and all of the equipment surrounding it, I could tell instantly that this was an operating room. I staggered back into the main room.

I shook my head firmly as Jocelyn eyed me with a frown. "I'm not stepping into that room until you tell me exactly what you want to do to me."

Jocelyn heaved a sigh, with an almost weary look on her face. She reached into the pocket of her lab coat and withdrew a gun. She aimed it at me.

"Look, Alice," she said. "I don't want to have to threaten you like this. Just step inside. I promise, this won't hurt."

If there was one thing I possessed, it was speed. And Jocelyn didn't exactly strike me as the most athletic of sorts, especially in her clackety heels. Likely, I could dodge beneath the tables out of view quicker than she even managed to pull the trigger of the gun. But that thought only brought me back to the same question as before. Where would I go? Even if I managed to outpace her and avoid getting hit by a bullet, I was trapped in the midst of a colony of hunters.

But I simply couldn't hand myself over to her like this. As futile as trying to escape would be, I wouldn't willingly step in that room. They would have to drag me in there kicking and screaming. I had the right to know what they were going to do to my body, dammit. I was not an animal to be herded from place to place and probed all they wanted. And I would fight to not be treated like one.

I took a gulp and met her eyes steadily.

Would she really attempt to shoot me? I knew by now that they saw value in me as a half-blood. It seemed that I was the first half-blood they had ever come across, and consequently I was also rare. But I didn't have time to debate the matter. I had made up my mind.

Before Jocelyn could react, quick as a flash, I'd ducked beneath the table behind me.

"Alice!" Jocelyn's voice echoed around the lab.

Keeping down low, I scrambled across the floor from table to table, winding through the maze toward the door which led to the staircase.

Her footsteps sped up across the room. By the sound of it, Jocelyn had removed her heels and she was running fast, faster than I'd expected.

But she couldn't come close to my speed. I had already reached the exit and launched myself down the stairs by the time she'd made it quarter way across the room. I sped up, leaping three steps at a time, wondering as I did why they didn't have a damn elevator running through this lab when they seemed to have them everywhere else. I'd almost reached the last flight of stairs when, turning the corner, I collided with someone. I was knocked backward, landing on my backside painfully against the sharp steps. My eyes shot upward. It was Mark. And approaching behind him were six other hunters.

I had not heard Jocelyn sound any alarms yet, and from the look of surprise in Mark's eyes as he stared down at me, I guessed that he and his companions had already arranged with Jocelyn to meet us up in the lab. What else would they be doing climbing up these stairs at this time in the morning?

Which meant… what exactly? *What were they planning to do to me in that operating room that required all of them to be present?*

Mark, along with the men behind him, drew out a gun. My attempt at escape had been even more short-lived than I had feared. Desperation overcoming all logic and caution, I hurled myself down the stairs. Even though they barricaded it, I hoped that the shock of my throwing myself toward them while they held loaded guns would work to my advantage.

And it did, but not enough. One of the men recovered from the surprise and he leapt at me. As he fell to the ground, his hands closed around my ankles, causing me to trip and crash down against the steps. I would have knocked my teeth out had I not instinctively put my hands out to shield my face in the fall.

"Let go of me!" I grunted, trying to wriggle away from him. I was almost successful, until the other men caught up with us and swooped down on me. When Mark approached and pressed his gun firmly against my neck, I knew that the game was over.

They quickly secured my hands behind my back with cuffs, and then they bound my feet. They carried me fighting and squirming back up the steps and into the lab. Jocelyn trailed behind us, her heels clutched in one hand.

"Convenient timing," she murmured to one of the hunters.

They marched me back to the operating room and wrestled me down onto the table, where they secured me with metal restraints.

"No!" I yelled. My back arched, the muscles in my arms and legs straining as I tried to break free. But whatever these restraints were made from, they were impervious to my strength. A sweat broke out on my forehead. "What do you want with me?" I panted.

The hunters' mouths remained closed in hard lines as they

finished securing me in place.

And then, perhaps all too predictably, one of them reached for a syringe and sank it deep into my neck.

Chapter 13: Julie

I thanked my lucky stars when we finally arrived at Uma's island. As we entered shallow waters, again, Aisha insisted that I handle the box myself. I hauled it off the boat and managed to pull it onto the sand without getting it too wet.

Aisha joined me next to the container. I gazed up at the sloping hill, at the top of which stood a castle—the witch's medical center. I already guessed that Aisha expected me to drag the box all the way up there by myself. This was just her wanting to inflict suffering on me, because she could have easily used her powers. Wasting time waiting for me to lug this thing up the hill was just plain stupid. But even aside from that, I had another incentive for wanting to do things a different way.

"It's going to take far too long," I dared to complain. "Let me go and get the witch. I'll try to convince her to come down here." I eyed the jinni cautiously.

Aisha paused, then to my relief, she nodded. "I'll wait here by the box. But don't take too long, or I'll come after you."

"Okay," I said, thankful that she had agreed without fuss. Aisha waiting here was best for many reasons. For one, the presence of the jinni would only get the witch's guard up and make it more difficult for me to persuade her. Aisha was so prickly, I was sure that one misplaced comment from either of them would blow the whole deal.

Secondly, and more importantly, I would be freer to steer things in the direction that I needed them to go without the jinni breathing down my neck and listening in on every word I spoke during the initial meeting… assuming I was even going to be able to get one.

Before heading off, I waded into the ocean to wash away the worst of the filth from my body, so that the witch wouldn't slam the door in my face in disgust the moment she opened it. Then, even as it pained me to leave Braithe alone with Aisha, I turned my back on her and the ocean and began racing up the hill toward the witch's medical center.

It was early in the morning. I guessed that the witch sisters would be asleep. I hoped that they wouldn't be too angry at my disturbance.

Arriving in front of the castle, I moved cautiously toward the front door. I placed my ear against the wood, listening for any sounds indicating that someone was awake inside. All was quiet. Waves crashed against the shore in the distance.

I knocked loudly, five times, then waited for several moments. I took a step backward, craning my neck to look up at the tall building. All the windows were dark, which worried me. I hoped they were home. And I didn't want to be forced to break in to verify it. It would make my task of convincing her to help us ten times more difficult. I knocked again, and waited some more.

From the corner of my eye, I caught a light flickering on in one of the downstairs windows. *Yes!*

Footsteps sounded on the other side of the door, which swung open. Standing before me could only have been Uma, the witch doctor herself. She bore much resemblance to her sister, who acted as her receptionist and whom we had met before. She shared the same bouncy auburn hair, light blue eyes and rounded features, although she was taller and more slender in build than her sister. She wore a purple velvet nightgown and her long hair was bound in a braid that hung down one shoulder.

Her brows furrowed as she looked down at me. "Who are you?" she asked. "And what brings you here at such an early hour?"

Although I had visited her castle with Benjamin, Arron, and Aisha, due to my getting rid of the merflor, we hadn't actually met the doctor herself. Only her sister.

Now that she stood before me—clearly I'd woken her up—I'd expected her to sound more irritated. She just seemed mildly surprised. "My name is Julie," I said. "Julie Duan."

I took a moment to shoot a glance behind me, anxious that Aisha might be stalking me, wanting to listen in on my conversation with the witch. But it was just my paranoia. I could make out her form still hovering on the beach in the distance, next to the white box. And something told me that she would remain at the beach and wait for my return, because jinn avoided witches like the plague—and vice versa. The only reason Aisha had ever agreed to Arron's idea of letting the witch operate on Benjamin before was that she had believed that there was absolutely no other way to release him from the Elder's curse.

My eyes returned to Uma, then darted over her shoulder toward the inside of the building. "I'm very sorry to disturb you at this rude hour, but may I come in? I have a very...

urgent situation."

The witch stiffened, looking me over with slight suspicion, but then she took a step back and opened the door wider for me to enter. After entering, she closed the door behind me and led me across the entrance hall to a door behind the desk where her sister usually sat. She opened it, and we emerged in what appeared to be her potion room. It was huge—far larger than even the spacious entrance hall— and there was barely an inch of the walls that wasn't covered by shelves filled with bottles of exotic-looking substances.

She led me over to a small table and gestured that I pull up a chair. We sat down opposite each other.

Clasping my sweaty hands together, I began, "I've discovered what I believe is a new species of supernatural… And you're the only person I could think of who could help in understanding what it is exactly."

She stared at me, disbelieving. "A new species? Where and what?"

I began to describe to the best of my ability the characteristics of the creatures, based on my observations of them so far, as well as the meager scraps of information the Elder had thrown us. By the time I was finished, the witch's mouth was practically hanging open. "You're joking with me," she said.

I shook my head. "I swear to you, I'm not here to waste your precious time," I said, looking earnestly into her blue eyes. "Besides, you don't need to believe me—I can show you."

"And where did you say you found them?" she pressed.

I hadn't said yet. I'd been skirting around the subject until now. "I got stranded with a friend in the ocean—long story—and we found them aboard a ship. My friend got taken by them and turned, leaving me alone. As I mentioned, I have brought a specimen to show you and will happily hand this over to you for inspection, but I must ask for something in exchange."

I could see from the look on her face that by now I'd perked the witch's interest enough to be able to demand my own terms. I hadn't been sure exactly how she would take to this information about the Bloodless, but it seemed that she was truly passionate about her profession and the discovery of a new species was both exciting and valuable to her.

"What do you want?" she asked, sitting up straighter in her chair. "Are you ill in some way?"

"I'm not ill," I said, even as I wished that in this myriad of bottles surrounding me there was a cure for broken hearts. "I have three requests to make of you. First, I want you to examine the creature I have brought here and, to the best of your medical knowledge, tell us how you think this species could be killed. Second, after you have examined the specimen, I want you to help exterminate the ship that is filled with these monsters… except for three of them, which I will select. These three are not to be harmed, which brings me to my third request: after we have exterminated the rest, I want you to bring those I've chosen back here to your island, keep them somewhere safe, and try to find a cure for them."

There was a span of silence as she took in my words.

"A cure?" She looked worryingly dubious about this.

"Yes," I said, gazing at her hopefully. "If you can't find a cure, then I don't know who will be able to… But even if you aren't able to find a cure, I need you to promise me that these four will remain safe."

There was another agonizing pause before she nodded her head slowly. "All right," she murmured. "You take me to this new species and be clear about those you wish me to take under my wing, and I will do so. In truth, despite the devastation you've described these 'Bloodless' are capable of wreaking, I'm more interested in examining them and taking samples for research than slaughtering them all outright."

"Good," I said, breathing out. I wasn't sure exactly how many minutes had passed since leaving Aisha, or even what the impatient jinni considered as "too much time", but I didn't want her coming after me before I'd managed to seal the deal with the witch. Aisha was already suspicious of me. I needed to speed up. "Now, the specimen I have brought for you is locked in a box, down on your shore near the harbor." I hesitated, bracing myself for what I had to tell her next. "The thing is, I'm not here alone. I'm here with a jinni."

The witch's face instantly soured. "What are you doing with a jinni?"

Getting into the full history of how we met would be wading into uncomfortable and dangerous waters, especially because some of that history involved me murdering Arron—who had apparently been a good acquaintance of the witch. I was sure that she wouldn't take kindly to the news that I'd slit his throat on her very own beach.

So rather than explain the whole saga, I simply said, "Let's just say that I owe her a favor… But for the most part, she is working for the same thing that we will be. She wants to stop the infestation and nip it in the bud before it continues to spread. I'm certainly not ignorant of the discord that exists between your kind and jinn, and I'll try to prevent her from getting in your way as much as I can…" I paused, swallowing hard. "There is one thing that I must mention though. She doesn't know that four of them used to be close companions of mine and, for reasons that would take me too long to explain, I can't reveal this to her. If I did, she'd likely target them first."

Of course, Aisha already knew about Arletta, but at least the jinni was still oblivious to the brothers… As long as she remained ignorant of who they were, they wouldn't be specifically targeted by her. They would just be three more pale faces among the crowd of Bloodless.

"I will point them out to you discreetly," I continued, "and it should look like they are your own selection of Bloodless you wish to examine, completely uninfluenced by me. One of the four is Braithe—whom I have brought with me here as the specimen."

This third request of mine thankfully worked to my advantage. The witch was naturally against anything that the jinni was for, so it wasn't difficult to persuade her to agree to help me preserve Hans' siblings.

Hans. I thought of him still stuck in that horrid cave back in Cruor, along with yet another crowd of Bloodless. They were, in fact, the original Bloodless. If they ever got out, they could start spreading another epidemic, but… until somebody went and let them out, I didn't see how they would escape. God knew their prison was well hidden. When

I'd first discovered that Hans was being held prisoner by the Elders after the war between Cruor and Aviary, I had scoured the entire realm for days on end. I would never have found the cave if one of the Elders had not escorted me there.

Of course, I had not told Aisha about Hans, or the cave in Cruor that was filled with more Bloodless. And I certainly wasn't going to—I would tell neither her, nor the witch, unless there arose a specific reason to. My desperate hope was that the witch would keep Hans' siblings safe, that she would discover at least some form of cure for them that could bring them closer to their former selves, and that I would somehow rid myself of Aisha after the ship of monsters was destroyed so that I could go and reclaim Hans.

Together, the witch and I worked out a plan of action. She also asked me what she was to do with the siblings if, after her experimentation, she failed to find a cure for them. I didn't have an answer for her other than that they still should not be killed. I just wanted to take things one step at a time because I couldn't bear to consider the possibility that there might be no way out of this for them. For Hans. For us.

All my hopes hung on a cure.

Once I was satisfied that the witch and I saw eye to eye, I agreed to show her Braithe. And it was about time, too. I could just imagine the jinni seething with impatience as she stalked around on the beach.

Uma used her magic to transport us to the shore, where Aisha was hovering next to the box. Aisha cast me a dirty look, but she barely even glanced at the witch before averting her eyes away, as though the ocean was more interesting to her than what the witch had to say. I was glad. If Aisha wanted to be a cold fish and not even greet the witch, it only worked to my advantage.

We circled the box cautiously before I stopped in front of the lock and planted my hands against the lid. I could hear Braithe pounding against the walls, still fighting to get out.

"Be careful," I advised the witch. "These creatures are dangerous even to witches. As soon as I open the lid, paralyze him and take him back to the castle."

"All right," Uma muttered as she rolled up the sleeves of her nightgown.

"How long is this going to take?" Aisha mumbled.

"We're not sure yet," I replied, eyeing the witch. "First Uma needs to take him to the castle so she can examine him, see what's what and try to work out how we can kill the creatures."

"And this is in exchange for what exactly?" Aisha asked.

"For three samples of the species. Uma would like to

choose three others to bring back to her castle and experiment further on them for her own research and interest."

I paused, holding my breath, fearing yet more probing questions from Aisha. But the jinni fell silent again after that.

Steeling myself for what I was about to do, I gulped, my eyes falling to the lid of the box. Reaching inside my bra, I pulled out the key and unlocked it. The lid sprang open without my even touching it. Uma and I stumbled back across the sand as Braithe burst out like a jack-in-the-box. His back and chest were heaving, his expression the picture of utter fury.

"Paralyze him!" I hissed at the witch.

She hit him with a curse, and… nothing happened. He continued to lurch toward the witch and me. My heart palpitating, I staggered back with Uma. A surge of horror rose within me. *Oh God. Her magic doesn't work on him!*

Then, without warning, his body froze up midair, and he collapsed on the sand.

Recovering from the shock, I slowly approached and gazed down at him. His eyes were still open. He was still conscious, just devoid of motion. It seemed as though there had been a delay in the witch's magic getting through to him for some reason. That was rather worrying, considering that we were relying on the witch's magic for everything regarding these creatures, but I comforted myself that she had managed to get through to him in the end. It had only taken a few extra seconds.

The witch's expression was a mix of horror and childlike fascination as she bent over Braithe's form and gazed down at him. After several moments of staring, she glanced up at me and nodded. "I don't know what you want to do while I'm working—wait here or in the waiting room back in the castle—but I can't yet give you an estimate of how long I'll be… This is going to take some time."

CHAPTER 14: JULIE

I ended up staying on the beach with Aisha. I would have preferred to wait in Uma's entrance hall simply because it was closer to where she was taking Braithe, but Aisha wanted to remain here—and this time she insisted that I stay with her.

Since the sun was on the verge of rising, I asked Uma to cast a spell of shade over me so that I wouldn't get burned. She agreed and then vanished with the rigid Braithe.

Aisha spun around and glared at me. "I hope you're not trying anything behind my back with this witch."

I froze. Did she know? Had she eavesdropped on our conversation after all?

If she had, then she already knew all about my plan, but

if she hadn't, I had everything to lose by coming out with the truth. It only made sense to keep lying. Besides, it wasn't even a big lie. I did genuinely want to stamp out this infestation before it spread further... I just wanted to save my loved ones in the process. The only loved ones I had left in the world. Was that really such a crime? Wouldn't Aisha or anyone with a beating heart do the same? I rationalized that even Benjamin would, if he were in my shoes.

"What do you mean?" I asked, my eyebrows knotting in a frown.

"I mean that you're a slimy little snake," she replied, eyeing me as though I was a cockroach she wanted to squish.

I scowled at her. I figured that acting offended was the best way to play my cards. "Well, I'm not trying anything other than what we discussed. You know that the supernatural realm has been my home for decades. Do you really think that I don't care about what happens to it?"

She smirked. "Is that even a question? You didn't seem too concerned about the safety of the supernatural realm when you went and delivered Benjamin right to the Elders' doorstep. Where was your solidarity then?"

At this, I stalled. She had a point, of course. I knew what a risk I'd posed to not only the supernatural realm but also the human realm. But... I'd been numb to the consequences of my actions. Nobody else could understand why I'd done what I'd done because nobody else understood the kind of love I held for Hans. My actions had been mad. Selfish. Even downright evil. But the truth was, I would do it all over again if it gave me the chance to be reunited with the love of my life. When I was still a human, he'd become my only reason for living and even after nearly two decades of being apart— hell, even now, after he'd turned into a creature of nightmares—he still was.

I cleared my throat and as I spoke, my voice was several tones deeper. "You're right. That was a monstrous thing of me to do. I'm not even going to try to justify it."

"Then why did you do it?" the jinni snarled.

I heaved a sigh. I couldn't tell her about Hans, of course— I needed to keep him undiscovered for as long as I could. My mind worked furiously trying to come up with some kind of rational explanation.

"I've been a victim of the Elders for almost as long as I can remember," I said, adopting a pained expression. "My entire life was destroyed by them. They took my family from me, my husband, and even my young child. I've spent decades living in fear of them, waking up each day terrified about what they had in store for me next." I paused to make a show of swallowing hard, as though just the memory of it was making me choke up. "Then one day, one of the Elders came to me with a proposition. None other than the feared Basilius himself. He told me that he had been privy to a prophecy by an oracle that indicated Benjamin Novak would be the one to help them recover after the war with the Hawks. He wanted my help in procuring Benjamin. He said that if I succeeded, once they came to power again, I would be treated with respect. I would be given power, and even freedom if I wished it. It was an offer that I just couldn't refuse."

Aisha frowned. "But they lost control of you after the war with the Hawks. The Elders were no longer powerful enough to control any of their vessels. You were already a free woman. Why would this offer even interest you?"

"That's true," I said, trying not to miss a beat. "But I was convinced that they would rise to power again, with my help or without, and then they would reclaim all their lost vessels. I believed I would be thrust back into the same miserable existence I'd endured for so long. So I... I decided to safeguard my future by offering to help them."

Aisha's lips parted in a grimace. "You disgust me," she murmured.

You're not exactly my favorite person either, I thought bitterly.

I knew that I ought to avoid hot buttons with Aisha but, perhaps because of how smoothly my meeting with the witch had gone, and her quick agreement to help me, I was experiencing a surge of confidence. I dared lash back a little at the jinni, if only to soothe my ego.

"And what of you? Weren't you essentially holding Benjamin as a prisoner, a lifelong slave to The Oasis?"

Aisha's eyes flashed, and I knew already that I'd gone too far again in mentioning Benjamin's name.

"We were his guardians!" she hissed. "He was a part of our family, and we were to protect him with our very lives. Something that a selfish, deceitful coward like yourself would never do for anyone." She paused, her eyes narrowing, before cutting me deeper. "I doubt you'd even do that for your own child if you had one."

Anger bubbled up within me, as well as righteous indignation. If only she knew the lengths that I was willing to go to for the man I loved. At the end of the day, the only difference between the jinni and me was that we loved different people. She and her family had apparently loved and accepted Benjamin as their own, and they were working to do everything they could to protect him, while I loved Hans and was doing the same for him. And I had experienced firsthand just how ruthless Aisha could be in that protection. Back when we had first met with Arron on that small island, if Benjamin hadn't stopped her, she would've killed me right then and there to use my heart for him. Then, she hadn't even known that I was working against Benjamin's best interests. In her eyes at that time, I'd been innocent.

Still, I held back on saying more. What use would bickering with this jinni do other than sink me deeper into the mud? I fell silent, pursing my lips and averting my attention to the ocean. I took in a deep breath and turned my thoughts to other things. Like how I was going to rid myself of the jinni after we had dealt with the ship of Bloodless. She'd made it clear that she was only keeping me alive because I was assisting her in this task. I was certain that she was going to try to murder me after that. I would have to beg the witch for protection—but I just hoped that the jinni's magic would not overpower the witch's. I was beginning to regret not adding a fourth request to my list for the witch doctor—to protect me from Aisha—but I was afraid to ask for too much at once.

I would have to hope that her inbuilt dislike for jinn would make her side with me rather than Aisha. Although both were wielders of magic, they worked in different ways and had completely different methods of manipulating their power. But from what I understood, jinn usually had the upper hand over witches.

Aisha wandered away from me, further up the shore, which I was glad about. That left me alone, with the box— still stained with the werewolf corpse's grime. Being stuck on the beach at the jinni's insistence and having nothing else to do, I decided to clean it. I dragged the box into the waves and submerged it, dipping down and using my hands as scourers to remove all the dirt. Despite the shadow the witch had cast over me, the sun was still bright in my eyes as it glistened off the surface of the waves. I had to squint to see what I was doing. Once the box was clean, I returned it to the beach and then waded back into the ocean to clean myself. I had rinsed myself off before but somehow, I still felt dirty.

I wasn't sure how much time passed, but the jinni and I stayed on separate parts of the beach, although I did notice her keeping an eye on me, shooting a glare over her shoulder every now and then.

Never mind the Bloodless, I wish I knew how to murder jinn.

From what I was able to pick up while traveling with them, it appeared that Aisha had a crush on Benjamin. I guessed that this was one of the reasons why she was so defensive of him. Maybe she'd even been in love with the vampire, despite him clearly not returning her advances in the slightest. He'd already told me that his heart was set on a girl back on his island. River, he'd said her name was.

I sank down on the sand, stretching out my legs, allowing the waves to wash over my feet and ankles.

I certainly couldn't blame the jinni for crushing on Benjamin. Aside from his uncommon good looks, his strength of character and unwavering bravery could easily make a girl fall for him. I wondered whether, if my heart hadn't already belonged to Hans, I might've fallen for him too.

But I would never live in a world where that was the case, because Hans owned me. Now and forever.

"Julie," Uma called, startling me. I shot to my feet and whirled around to see that she had arrived on the sand just behind me. She had changed out of her nightclothes and was wearing a long brown dress. Wrapped around her was an apron which, to my discomfort, appeared to be stained with blood. Braithe might not have had blood of his own, but after the feasting on that small island, I was sure that he still must've had some of his victims' blood left in his system. My pulse quickened as I feared she might've gone back on her word to do nothing to harm him.

Apparently she noticed my unease. She said beneath her

breath, "Don't worry. He's all right."

Her eyes shifted from me further along the beach. Following her gaze, I caught sight of Aisha moving toward us. She had spotted Uma already.

"So what happened?" I asked anxiously.

"I suggest you come with me to my treatment room. Your jinni friend can come, too."

"Not my friend," I muttered.

Aisha arrived next to us, for the first time laying eyes on Uma for more than a few seconds at a time.

"Well?" she asked, eyeing the witch expectantly. "What did you discover?"

This was also the first time that she had directly addressed the witch since arriving on the island. I guessed that she really was fed up with waiting and just wanted to get this task over with.

Uma eyed her. "I suggest that you both come up to my castle. That'll be a more suitable place to talk than down here."

I turned on Aisha and raised a brow. "I guess you'll be waiting here again?"

"No, I'll come with you," she huffed.

"Okay," I said, even as disappointment clawed at my chest. What I really wanted to know was whether the witch had managed to gain an idea of how to cure the Bloodless. But with Aisha present, we would only be able to discuss Uma's findings on how to murder them. I would need to find another opportunity to ask her about the cure— perhaps, once we arrived at the ship, we would find a moment when Aisha was distracted.

I looked back down in the box. This wasn't a private island. Although it belonged to the witch sisters, Uma had many visitors—a myriad of supernaturals who wanted treatments of various illnesses.

"If Aisha is coming with us this time," I said, "I don't want to leave this box alone here on the beach. It's a… special type of box and it has a lot of value to me."

"Not a problem," the witch replied. With a click of her fingers, the box vanished. "I transported it up to the castle, behind the desk in the waiting room. It will be safe there. Nobody will touch it."

"Thank you," I said.

I approached Uma and reached out to touch her so that she could vanish me up to the castle. Seconds before she vanished us, Aisha whizzed toward me and grabbed hold of my other arm. We disappeared, the jinni allowing the witch's magic to flow through her and transport her with us. This took me by surprise. A jinni willingly submitting to the magic of a witch? I didn't know an awful lot about the jinn, but I was certain that this was unheard of. Was she really too lazy to travel on her own strength? It made me recall how reluctant she had been to offer me any help with the box, and back on the ship when she had used me as a guinea pig to attack the Bloodless. The most strenuous thing she had done to help me then had been to lift me away from danger. Had making me face the danger while she watched really all only been about exacting revenge on me?

These behaviors combined made me wonder whether this jinni really was as strong as she made herself out to be. She had recently spent a lot of time within Benjamin fighting off the Elder. I wondered whether that was having an impact on her strength.

But again, I didn't have much time to ponder this as we arrived in the witch's treatment room, which looked very much like the potion room I'd met her in earlier to talk. This one also had countless bottles of ingredients lining shelf upon shelf against the wall, each one labeled neatly and clearly—most of whose names I couldn't even pronounce. But in the center of this room was a long, metal examination table, upon which lay Braithe. His wrists and ankles had been strapped to steel posts at each corner of the table, and he was lying there, stretched out and unmoving. His eyes were closed. Again, a horrible doubt filled my mind that the witch could have deceived me. I moved closer to examine him. Yes, he was breathing. He was alive—or as alive as he could be in his present state. He just appeared to be in a deep slumber, perhaps also still in the state of paralysis the witch had put him under earlier with her magic.

The witch cleared her throat. "So," she began, folding one arm over the other as she stood at the foot of the treatment table. Her eyes roamed the length of Braithe's naked, emaciated form. "I have completed a preliminary examination. It has by no means given me conclusive answers, but I'm in a position to be able to make some educated guesses."

"Please," I said, "just tell us everything that's going through your mind—even if you're not sure it's true."

"I'm sure that these creatures can be killed, just like regular vampires such as yourself can," the witch said to me. "They possess, after all, physical bodies." She reached for a container on the counter that was filled with sharp knives—presumably for dicing up ingredients—and picked one up. Hovering the knife over Braithe's right hand, she slid the edge of the blade against the tip of his forefinger, creating a small slit in his skin no larger than a paper cut.

Braithe remained just as unconscious, and not even the

smallest tinge of blood emerged from the cut. The wound remained dry, almost brittle.

Uma replaced the knife on the counter before continuing, "The body of a human-turned-vampire such as yourself, if left without blood for too long, can start to morph and mutate into something different. Quite different."

"But not all of those creatures on the ship were starved of blood," Aisha said, frowning. "I saw with my own eyes how perfectly normal vampires were turned by the Bloodless into one of them in a matter of hours."

"Correct," Uma said. "Originally, there was a vampire, possibly even more than one, who got deprived of blood for too long. In the process of their bodies adapting to survive without blood, they still retained the vampiric ability to turn... except now, their victims take the form of their new evolved bodies."

There was a span of silence as Aisha and I waited with bated breath for the witch to continue.

"Regarding the 'original' Bloodless, so to speak," Uma said, "I imagine that during the earlier days of blood deprivation—the first few months perhaps, maybe even up to a year, depending on how recently they'd last fed—their bodies consumed their own blood for preservation... In time, when no new blood was consumed, the body had to start finding another way to survive. What you see here"—she eyed the length of Braithe—"is nature's answer. A body that craves blood more than anything else... but that no longer requires it to function."

My mouth hung open as I gazed at her, enraptured, scared to miss even a single word.

"What about Derek Novak?" Aisha asked the witch. "You must know of the legendary ruler of The Shade. He survived four hundred years without blood, and he didn't turn into one of these things."

"I am aware of that vampire's case," the witch replied. "But he had the assistance of a witch at the time— a witch who cast a sleeping spell upon him, that would have also served to preserve his body."

"Hm," Aisha murmured.

"I haven't examined this one internally yet," Uma went on, eyeing Braithe again, "so I can't go into precise details regarding how his body is able to function exactly, but I think I've gleaned enough to help wipe out the ship..." Uma's eyes fell on me. I guessed that she would need to cut Braithe open at some point, especially if she was ever going to find a cure. I hoped that she wouldn't make a mistake in the procedure and end his life accidentally.

"You mentioned, Julie," the witch continued, "that you

already tried to stake a Bloodless through the heart—perhaps the most common way to kill a vampire. I think I know the reason why that doesn't work. As I'm sure you're aware, when a human is turned by a normal vampire, the vampiric infection is transferred through the blood and settles in the heart first and foremost—that is where the nature of the Elder takes root, which gradually affects the rest of the body physically. But in the case of the Bloodless, based on the fact that staking the heart doesn't kill them, I'm taking a guess that the absence of blood has caused the original infection's concentration in the heart to break down and infuse the entire body."

Aisha shook her head and held up a hand. "Wait, you're losing me. I know that a vampire's immortality is due to the Elders' nature infecting their heart—which is why destroying the heart also destroys the immortality—but if in the case of the Bloodless the Elders' nature has dissipated from the heart due to lack of blood, wouldn't that make the Bloodless more vulnerable? More mortal, not stronger?"

"You're right in a way," Uma replied. "The vampiric infection that causes immortality still exists in them, but it is broken down and leaked throughout the body which simply means that no particular part of the body is especially vulnerable. You have to strike in multiple places to end them—for example, chop them to pieces so that they can no longer physically move."

There was a pause as Aisha and I let Uma's words sink in.

Aisha crossed her arms over her chest. "What I don't understand is how an original Bloodless could even come about. How long would they need to starve in order to reach this state?"

"Taking a wild guess, I would say at least six years," the witch replied. I was grateful that Aisha had no way of knowing the real truth of how the original Bloodless came about, my own Hans being part of the group.

"I don't get how a vampire could in reality be deprived of blood for so long," Aisha continued. "I can't imagine why he or she would not have at least been able to procure some animal blood."

Uma shrugged. "I don't know how the original Bloodless came to be. That's a mystery yet to be unraveled."

"Back to the topic of killing them," I said to the witch, eager for a change of subject. "Please tell us more."

"Yes," the witch replied. "If you want to kill one of these, I believe that you will need a razor sharp blade—sharper than what you tried using— and you will need to sever the body in several spots… for example, chop off the head, sever the midriff, and perhaps also the legs. I'm afraid that I'm not aware of the extent of their bodies' healing capabilities, but they certainly do not appear to be as fast as a regular vampire's."

Another silence engulfed us as the three of us glanced over Braithe's form again.

I wished once more in frustration that Uma could just tell me what ideas she'd come up with regarding a cure. I could hardly bear to look at Braithe like this. I just wanted him back. I wanted Hans back. I wanted all of them back. I wanted my life back. *Is that really so much to ask for?*

"Well," Aisha muttered, interrupting the quiet, "that's what this specimen here is for. We can test your speculations right now."

Before either the witch or I could react, the jinni had shot toward the counter where Uma had left the knife. Swiping it, she shot back to the examination table.

I wanted to scream at the jinni to step away, but I managed to restrain myself. Such a reaction would be far too much of a giveaway.

"Wait, Aisha," I said, fighting to adopt a steady tone of voice. I reached out and closed my hand around hers and gently pushed the knife downward.

"For what?" she snapped.

"We don't even know if Uma has finished with her

experimentation on this one yet," I said, the words flying from my lips as I thought of them. "Shouldn't we ask? She might have more things to explain to us first."

Aisha turned on the witch. "Well, do you?"

"I do, actually," the witch replied calmly. She walked over to Aisha and took the knife from her hand. She set it back down on the table behind her. "In fact," Uma continued, "I would rather that we don't kill this one in particular. I'm in the process of a number of experiments. I've already pumped his body with a couple of potions."

Aisha grumbled, but didn't insist. I let out a quiet sigh of relief.

"So how exactly do you propose that we storm the ship?" I asked. "We need a lot of sharp blades. That's it? Couldn't you use your magic to get rid of them?"

"Yes," Uma said, "I could certainly attempt to slice through them with my magic. As you noticed when I stunned this one with a spell, they aren't instantly receptive to witch magic—at least, there's a small delay, which is another reason to have you by my side assisting me. I'm still not quite sure as to why a delay is there, that's something I have yet to find out... How many did you say were on that ship?"

"I haven't counted exactly," I admitted, "but it looked like there were over sixty… at least. They might've even reached some other island by now and turned more vampires to join them."

"All right," she said, standing up and walking over to a counter in the corner of the room. It was only now that I noticed a steaming black cauldron on full heat. She stood before it and stirred it with a large ladle. Picking up a glass vial, she tipped a spoonful of dark gray liquid into it before bringing it over to us. "This is a tranquilizer I've managed to develop in the past few hours that I believe will work on these creatures."

"Okay…" I murmured, eyeing the concoction.

"I will equip you with blow darts tipped with this potion. You have to shoot the dart into the creatures—preferably their throats, although other parts of the body will do—and make sure that it penetrates the skin. The poison should cause their bodies to go into paralysis for at least two or three hours. So when we arrive at the ship, after I have singled out a few to keep for my own research, we will start work on the creatures. I suggest that the first thing you do is try to slice them in three places as I have described simply because this is the fastest method. But if you're finding yourself in a particularly difficult situation, use one of the darts to tame them first."

I breathed out. "Good," I said. I liked the idea of the paralyzing darts. Knowing that I was equipped with them would definitely offer some reassurance when down there fighting with those lethal creatures.

"Will there be a delay in this potion getting through to them?" I asked.

"A delay of a few seconds," she replied. "I already tested the potion on this creature here. I brought him out of my paralyzing spell and then shot him with one of the darts—in the throat." I scanned Braithe's neck, where the skin seemed to be particularly thin and almost translucent. "You won't see the mark now," Uma added. "It's had time to heal. Anyway, the potion took approximately five point five seconds to take effect on him. Then he drifted off into a deep slumber."

"What's all that blood on your apron?" Aisha asked the witch, wrinkling her nose.

"The blood of the last victim he consumed," she replied grimly. "I had to make several iterations of this potion because the first few caused him to throw up. I'm sure he expelled almost all of the blood in his system. Now he is quite pale again, as you can see."

"All right," Aisha said. "We should return to the ship." She paused, her eyes settling on Braithe's face. "But isn't it a risk keeping Bloodless alive here? It only takes one of them to break free from your castle to recreate the problem we have now."

Uma shook her head. "You need not worry about that, jinni," she replied. "This specimen and the ones I choose from the vessel will be kept securely locked away. And once I'm finished with my experimentation, I will end their lives."

That seemed to satisfy Aisha, or at least enough that she didn't argue further.

The witch returned to her cauldron filled with tranquilizer potion and turned off the heat. "The two of you can go wait outside in the entrance hall. I will bring you everything we need."

Aisha and I looked at each other, then respected the witch's request. Perhaps she wanted some time alone to clear her head before we descended on the ship. Although it pained me to leave Braithe as he was, stark naked and stretched out on the treatment bed like a cadaver, I trusted Uma enough to believe that she would put him away somewhere safe, and keep him safe while we were gone.

Aisha and I didn't exchange a word as we sat together in the entrance room, but the witch didn't leave us alone long. She emerged carrying two bulging grey shoulder bags and four long, sheathed swords. She approached us and handed one of the bags to me, along with two of the swords. Then she turned to Aisha, giving her the other bag and the other two swords. I winced. Surely, this was a direct insult to the jinni, who should not require the use of crude weapons and brute force to end the Bloodless. But strangely, Aisha did not act offended. Rather, she accepted the witch's offerings without a word.

I looked down into my own bag to see that it was heaped with feather-ended blow darts. Beside them, in a thin, long inner compartment of the bag, was the blowgun itself—smaller than I'd expected it to be, and made of mahogany.

The witch now stood empty-handed. She would work only with her magic.

"Will your sister accompany us, too?" I asked.

"My sister is not home. She's visiting a relative."

"Oh, okay," I said, disappointed. It wasn't so much that I thought we couldn't handle the ship with the three of us, but I would have been comforted to have a second witch there as a barrier against Aisha in case she decided to murder me the moment we finished with the Bloodless. I would have begged both sisters to help me escape. They might even stick up for me, if only to behave contrary to the jinni. But there was only one witch—Uma. I had no choice but to rely on her.

"Let's go," Aisha pressed.

"All right," the witch said, a hint of apprehension in her eyes as she glanced at me. "Let's go."

CHAPTER 15: JULIE

For the second time, just before the witch vanished with me, Aisha reached out and clutched my arm, allowing herself to be transported by the witch's magic. When we reappeared, hovering over an endless expanse of waves near where we'd left my ship, I couldn't help but ask her why.

The jinni glowered at me and pursed her lips.

"Can either of you see the ship anywhere?" the witch asked.

I turned my attention to the matter at hand. Gazing around, I couldn't spot any sign of it.

"Are you certain we're in the right area?" the witch asked.

"Yes," Aisha replied, half confident, half impatient. "Let's keep moving."

The witch kept hold of me, allowing me to glide alongside her, while the jinni flew beside us by her own magic.

"Over there," Aisha said, after about five minutes of soaring and scanning the waves. She was pointing south of our position. "Do you see it?" she asked, squinting.

"Yes," the witch and I replied. Now that she'd pointed it out, I could see it. It was my boat—I could tell even from this far distance. We zoomed toward it with supernatural speed. When we arrived above the deck, it was empty except for the bloodied corpses of a few witches strewn about the deck. The absence of Bloodless up here shouldn't have been too much of a surprise, considering that it was daytime. Like regular vampires, I guessed that they weren't sun worshipers.

We touched down on the floorboards, near the broken trap door. My hand locked around the hilt of my sword as we carefully descended to the lower deck. My heart ached again at what a wreck it was. Gazing around, we moved along the corridor, searching each of the cabins… only to find that they were empty. We moved on to search the other levels of the ship. We didn't find a single Bloodless. The ship was still moving, but apparently, that was by the will of the sharks alone.

"What happened here?" I breathed. I couldn't understand

for the life of me where they could have all vanished to.

"Seems they've abandoned ship," Aisha murmured.

The witch furrowed her auburn brows. "Why would they do that?"

Aisha shrugged. "Let's keep moving. They can't have gotten too far. Maybe they took one of the lifeboats?"

"Even if they took all of the lifeboats, the Bloodless couldn't all have fit on them," I said, shaking my head.

We returned to the deck and checked the lifeboats all the same. There were three left in total. Only one was missing—the same one Aisha and I had taken to travel to Uma's island. We moved around the circumference of the ship, scanning the water surrounding us, but none of us spotted a surge of Bloodless swimming beneath the waves. We would need to leave the vessel and continue soaring over the ocean.

The witch carried me higher than she'd flown with me before, and the jinni followed suit. The higher up we were, the wider area we could scan at once.

We kept our eyes peeled for what felt like the next hour as we flew in search of the monsters, until we began reaching even deeper waters. Waters the Mansons and I had always tried to avoid due to the ghastly sea creatures that were rumored to inhabit them.

As we continued flying, I caught the sound of distant

shouts. Though it was more than shouts. It was deep, guttural roars.

I looked in the direction of the noise. A ship loomed on the horizon.

"Hurry," I said, pointing toward it.

As we neared the vessel, its features became clearer. Going by its heavy-handed construction and black sails, I guessed that it belonged to ogres. Maybe it was even the infamous *Skull Crusher* itself.

As we hovered over the deck, I let out a gasp. Beneath us was a scene of utter chaos. The roaring had been coming from ogres, lumbering around the deck, wielding axes and spears, as Bloodless tore into cell after cell of... humans.

Oh, God.

This must have been one of the ogres' cargo ships. Perhaps they'd come too near to the Bloodless on my ship, and, smelling the blood of humans, the Bloodless had leapt aboard.

The floor was scattered with humans, some writhing on the floor—apparently in transformation—while others appeared to be dead.

By the looks of it, the ogres weren't doing a good job at quelling the Bloodless' attack. The Bloodless were too agile and quick for the thundering ogres, and by the time the ogres had lurched toward them with an ax, the Bloodless had already darted in the opposite direction.

I was shocked to see that even ogres lay dead on the huge deck, while some were strewn in the ocean—in both cases, drenched in their own blood. It seemed that these creatures really would attack anything—humans, witches, ogres, werewolves...

"Okay," Uma said, her voice steady even in the midst of such carnage. "Before we float down, I will keep aside those I wish to use for my research, and then the rest can be finished off."

Aisha had already unsheathed a sword and was clutching it in her hands. It seemed that she really was going to use brute force in slaying these creatures rather than her magic.

I quickly scanned the vessel for Hans' siblings. In all the commotion that was going on, I couldn't spot them. They were all moving too fast in their massacre of the humans, and in the ogres' desperate attempt to stop them. The Bloodless were practically blurs of pallor whizzing about the deck.

"Well, come on then," Aisha complained. "Choose them and let's get this over with."

I caught sight of a group of Bloodless standing on one of the raised platforms, near the wheel of the ship. They were prowling around one of the still unopened cages of humans.

After verifying that none of them were Hans' siblings, I suggested to Aisha, "Well, we can start already, I guess." I pointed toward the crowd by the unopened cage. "Why don't we begin over there, and then Uma has the rest of the ship to choose her specimens from."

Aisha took the bait, and, with barely a backward glance to see if I was following her, she moved toward them with a murderous gleam in her eyes. The girl was mad, I was sure.

As she reached the crowd, she leapt toward one and brought her sword down against his neck. I should have immediately been focusing my attention on finding Colin, Frederick and Arletta, but I couldn't tear my eyes away. The first strike didn't sever his head. Neither did it sever the second or even third time. Only after the fourth strike did she finally manage to send his head rolling to the floorboards. No blood spilled, and his body keeled and collapsed in a heap. Aisha then began hacking at the rest of his body, as if she feared that it would rise again, headless.

I refocused my attention on my priority and swept my eyes once more around the deck from where I still hovered with the witch in the air. Finally, I spotted them. All three of them were huddled together in one corner, sharing a human amongst themselves. I found the sight bizarrely heartwarming. *At least they're sticking together.* I wondered if they recognized each other at all. Whether they could even experience finer emotions like love or attachment... or whether all they experienced was an all-consuming desire for what their bodies were incapable of holding in—blood.

Discreetly, I pointed the siblings out to the witch.

"That's them," I whispered.

"Just those three?"

"Yes," I said, taking a deep breath. "You need to make it look like you've just chosen those three on your own, randomly. And get them out of here."

"All right," she said. "I'll vanish with them back to my island. It'll only take a few moments, and then I'll return."

"Thank you," I said, my heart swelling with gratitude.

"I'll need to put you down somewhere first though," she murmured.

"Just"—my eyes traveled around wildly—"just drop me on that mast."

I wasn't as afraid for my safety now compared to before, not with the distraction caused by all this fresh human blood. But taking me to the mast I'd pointed to wasn't quite as simple as I'd anticipated. It was already occupied by a couple of Bloodless, perched among the sails, sucking on a human between them. The witch darted around with me until we found an empty mast where she could let go of me.

Balancing, I scanned the deck anxiously again to verify that Colin, Arletta and Frederick were still—

"Aisha!" A scream erupted from my throat.

In the short time that Uma and I had had our backs turned, she had abandoned the group of Bloodless that she had been working on near the wheel and had approached the siblings. Colin, Frederick and Arletta. They... they lay on the ground, decapitated. With blows so quick her hands were almost a blur, she was in the process of hacking the rest of their bodies into chunks.

I leaped from the safety of the mast, down to the blood-encrusted deck with a crash. I hadn't even considered the danger I was putting myself into. The witch also hurtled forward, but we were both too late.

No.

No!

I gazed with stunned eyes from the twitching pieces of the siblings' mangled bodies to Aisha. The jinni wiped sweat from her brow with the back of her hand, a look of satisfaction on her face.

"Did you call me?" she asked in an innocent voice, cocking her head to one side.

"You killed the wrong ones!" I screamed like a banshee. I fell to my knees and gazed in horror, barely believing my eyes.

"Oh, I'm so sorry," Aisha drawled. "I didn't realize…"

"You were supposed to start with those over there!" I bellowed, thrusting my finger toward the Bloodless she'd abandoned by the wheel, even as tears streamed down my cheeks.

I was blowing my cover, but I couldn't even care anymore. She already knew about what I'd planned. Somehow, she had figured it out.

I could no longer contain myself. I'd been through too much in too short a time. This was the final straw for me. I exploded. I barely even registered the words spilling from my mouth as grief consumed me. I hurled every curse word I knew at her before lunging toward the jinni with my sword drawn.

She swept up into the air, dodging my advance.

"So, the witch was going to save those three for you, was she?" Aisha asked as she hovered above me.

I lost the strength to even continue my attempts to attack her any more. I dropped the sword and sank back to the floor. My head thrust back, my face toward the heavens, I howled.

"Why did you do this?" the witch asked the jinni. "I was to take these three back with me. That was the deal."

The jinni stiffened. "Do you really think I'm that stupid? You're only choosing these three as a favor to Julie."

How did she find out? I could only guess that I'd underestimated her hearing.

Aisha swooped down on me, gripping my throat. She hauled me to my feet and then lifted me up into the air. Her eyes sparkled malevolently.

"I told you what would happen if you stepped out of line," Aisha hissed.

"Let go of her," the witch spoke up. "What harm has she done to you?"

Still retaining her grip on me, Aisha turned her glower on the witch.

"Oh, I'm afraid that she has done much harm. More harm, I suspect, than you're aware of. Clearly, the little snake didn't inform you of the destruction she almost brought upon the supernatural world." Aisha's thick jaws clenched hard. "And of what she did to a dear friend of mine."

The witch faltered. She frowned, her eyes falling on me, and raised a brow.

"Don't believe her!" I gasped, trying to pry myself free from the jinni's grasp. "She's lying. Please, help me!"

"Speaking of dear friends," Aisha continued, making my blood run cold, "she also murdered one of yours. Arron."

"Arron?" Surprise flashed in the witch's eyes.

"She murdered him on your very own beach."

"She's lying!" I screamed.

"She's the only liar here," Aisha replied, her fingernails digging into my flesh.

"You have to believe me," I breathed, looking desperately at the witch. "Please. Would you really trust a jinni over a vampire?"

There was doubt in Uma's eyes as she looked at me. Then, to my horror, she took a step back. Arron must've meant a lot to her for her to take a jinni's words so seriously. It seemed that the girl had shaken Uma enough to want nothing more to do with me.

But she still has Braithe in her castle!

"Wait! Please!"

"I-I'm sorry, Julie," Uma said, her voice deep. "I don't know which of you is telling the truth. You two clearly have—"

Her voice faltered as a violent tremor ran through the boat. While Aisha had by now pinned me against a mast, Uma had still been planted on the deck. The shudder made the witch lose her footing, and she fell to the floor. The boat tilted sharply and abruptly, sending the witch crashing along with several Bloodless against the railing of the ship. The next thing I knew, several gargantuan, reddish poles with speared tips thrust down from above. One pierced right through Uma's gut. I gasped, too stunned to scream. It had all happened so fast, I doubted she'd even had time to realize what was happening to her before it was too late.

The spell of shade the witch had cast to protect me from the sun vanished, plunging me into agony as rays touched me. The witch was dead.

Squinting through the sunlight and trying to get a handle on the burning sensation that erupted in my skin, I followed the poles upward with my eyes, only to realize that they weren't poles.

My heart stopped and my eyes bulged. I gaped up at what looked like a colossal crab, hanging over the edge of the ship. The middle of its body was a furious red, with two glossy black eyes set wide apart on either side of its head and terrifying pincers that clicked together. Three of its freakishly long, spear-like legs had crashed down over the side of the vessel as it clung on—one of which had ended the witch, while the others had speared through two Bloodless. The monsters' feet splintered the wooden floorboards as it heaved itself onto the deck, revealing a full set of eight such deadly legs. It let out a nasty screech that made my eardrums ache and raised its forelegs in the air. The legs that had pierced the witch and the Bloodless still had their bodies attached to them.

Horror rushed through me. I knew what these were. These were the legendary Great Sea Arachnids. Some called them water spiders, while others called them crabs, but they were rumored to live in these parts of the ocean. I shouldn't have been surprised at their arrival. They would have scented the dead bodies in the water.

Four more crabs scrambled up over the side of the ship. As their feet landed, a couple of them lodged through the bodies of Bloodless, skewering them on their long legs just as one had done to Uma. As they began to stomp down on anyone near them—ogres, Bloodless and humans—I realized that piling up bodies on each of their legs like barbecue sticks was how they caught their prey.

Even Aisha appeared to be frozen in shock. One of them lurched forward in our direction, extending its menacing pincers. Taking advantage of the precarious moment and the fact that Aisha was still in her physical form, I gripped her hands and sank my claws in them, forcing her to let go. I tumbled down to the deck amidst the chaos and threw myself beneath a pile of barrels.

I have to get away from this jinni.

Careful to stay close to the ground, and obscured by

barrels and upturned tables, I scrambled toward the edge of the boat—keeping myself hidden behind a high pile of rope—and looked downward. My breath hitched. The waves were swarming with the monsters, their bright red heads bobbing above the waves.

I glanced anxiously back over my shoulder in search of the jinni. I spotted her flitting about over the center of the deck. It wouldn't be long until she'd found me.

As my gaze fell back on the nightmarish arthropods, I had only two choices before me.

Get skewered alive by a hulking crab, or get caught by Aisha.

It actually wasn't such a hard decision to make.

Chapter 16: Julie

I tried to choose a spot to dive in that wasn't infested with the monsters. Crashing down into the waves, I prayed that I wouldn't collide headfirst with one of the crabs. I forced my eyes open, even as the salt stung. At least the daylight was more tolerable down here.

Chills ran through me as I spied several monsters just a dozen feet away, and many more rising up from the darkest depths of the ocean for their luncheon. My only ray of hope was that most of them seemed to be approaching the boat from its starboard side, while the area directly beneath the vessel, and also to the port, was less densely populated.

I swam directly beneath the shadow of the vessel, through

the gap between the keel and the rudder. So far, no crabs were making a show of moving toward me. All their focus seemed to be on the deck of the ship.

I drifted down deeper, at the same time backing away from the stream of crabs to my right. I had to get away from these waters as fast as I could. Aisha would no doubt check the surrounding waves once she'd verified I was no longer on the deck. Perhaps she'd started scouring the ocean's surface already.

As I descended, I continued eyeing the arthropods, terrified that one would suddenly take interest in me as an appetizer.

Streams of bubbles and a muffled scream escaped from my mouth as something sharp clamped around my right leg. My eyes shot down to see the jaws of a shark closing around my shin. My claws extended, I slashed at the shark's eyes, causing it to let go of me and back away in pain. It had reins attached to it. It was one of the sharks that pulled the ogres' ship. I had drifted too close to the vessel's bow.

The shark had cut two nasty gashes in my leg. They hurt like hell, but I was grateful at least that he hadn't torn my entire leg off.

A mad jinni, giant crabs, lethal sharks… I wondered how many more obstacles life could throw my way.

Haven't I suffered my fair share already? Wasn't losing Hans and his siblings enough?

I didn't think my heart could take any more nasty surprises.

Even as my right leg ached, I forced both of my legs into action, propelling me deeper. Keeping an eye on the stream of crabs rising to the surface, eventually I reached the last of the horde. There must have been at least fifty of them in total attacking the ship now.

I moved further away from the boat, maintaining my depth. I'd swum so deep by now, I was beginning to feel the pressure on my lungs. I'd need to resurface sometime soon, but not until I felt a safe distance away.

Constantly glancing over my shoulder as I swam, I sped forward for miles before finally allowing myself to surface for breath. The sun's rays touched me uninhibited. Wincing, I kept my head down low as I took in deep, steady breaths. I gazed back at the ship. In my panic, I'd swum further than I had expected. It was just a small fleck on the waves now. I couldn't spot the jinni, but I couldn't afford to become complacent either. As soon as I'd renewed my body with oxygen, I submerged myself in the ocean again and continued swimming away.

I wasn't sure what would happen to all those Bloodless

who'd been on the ogres' ship. It seemed that the spider crabs weren't exactly discriminatory about whom or what they caught. Maybe those creepy arthropods would do the job Uma, Aisha and I had set out to do—wipe the Bloodless out.

But I couldn't pay any thought to that now.

There was only one thing on my mind as I raced away: Braithe.

***

I wasn't even sure how I managed it, but I did. I found my way back to Uma's island alive. As I entered shallow waters and crawled out of the waves and onto the beach, a surge of relief rushed through me, despite the sun digging into me once again.

Barely taking a moment to catch my breath, I hurried away from the beach and raced up the hill to Uma's castle. This time, I didn't knock. Uma had already said that her sister was away visiting relatives. There would in theory be nobody at home... except for Hans' brother.

I kicked the door down with my supernatural strength and raced across the hallway and down a corridor, toward the treatment room where Braithe had been taken.

When I forced open the door, to my relief, he was still here. I'd half feared that Aisha might reach here before me, having guessed that Braithe, too, was somebody I loved.

Braithe lay naked on the treatment table, eyes closed. He was still asleep in what seemed to be the same position we'd left him in. His wrists and ankles were still restrained, and I guessed that the witch had probably pumped him with another few doses of her tranquilizer potion before she left.

I approached the bed cautiously and touched his cold, deathly pale face. As I gazed down at his freakish appearance, I tried to ignore what Braithe had become and notice only the shadows of his former features. The features that reminded me so much of his brother, Hans.

I couldn't waste any more time. Swallowing hard, I gazed about the room. A pile of drug-laced blow darts heaped on one of the counters caught my eye. I hadn't even gotten a chance to use the ones Uma had equipped me with, along with the blow gun. My memory was hazy as to at exactly which moment I'd lost them in the fray.

I swept all the darts off the counter and into an empty drawstring bag that hung from the back of a chair. I also spied another blow gun—two in fact. I took them and fastened both to my belt, just for good measure, along with a sword I found leaning against the wall. Then the only thing left for me to retrieve from this room was Braithe himself. I rummaged around for keys that would unlock Braithe's restraints, and found them hanging from a hook above the sink.

Still anxious that he might wake up again, I moved slowly and cautiously as I unclasped the cuffs. Then, holding both of his icy, bony hands, I tugged, pulling him into a sitting position. His head dropped and lolled over his chest. His slumber was definitely deep.

I dared slip one arm around his waist, and then hauled him off the table, supporting his body against me—no easy task for someone as short as myself. His legs ended up dragging on the floor as I hurried with him toward the exit, but there was nothing I could do to avoid it.

"It's okay, Braithe," I whispered, my voice choked as I thought of Frederick, Colin and Arletta. I would never even have the chance to attempt saving them. They were gone. "We'll sort you out."

I dragged him out of the castle and down the hill, toward the island's small harbor. The day was getting on, and although the sun was still agonizing, it wasn't quite as piercing as before. Still, it melted my flesh as we hurried down toward the jetty. There were several boats on each side. The one I ought to choose was clear—there was only one with a covering over it. Even though it was small, it would be better than nothing.

I pulled Braithe beneath the shelter of the vessel and tried to lay him down in a semi-comfortable position before moving to the bow. By a stroke of good fortune, there were already a couple of dolphins attached to the boat on a loose tether. I reeled them in and, clutching the reins tightly, sat down beneath the shelter.

We had our engine. Now we could flee.

Chapter 17: River

A bright light lit up the backs of my eyelids. As consciousness returned to my brain, I opened my eyes and sat up slowly. My vision was hazy at first, but even with impaired sight I could immediately tell that I was somewhere unfamiliar. First of all, I was lying in a bed. A proper bed, with a soft mattress—not like the operating table that I last remembered lying on. My vision came into focus. There was a white curtain drawn around the bed, enclosing me in my own private space.

"Hello?" I called, only realizing as I spoke just how parched and sore my throat was. A glass of water sat on top of a bedside table to my right. I reached for it and swallowed it in a few gulps. Then I swung my legs off the bed—or at least tried to. Shoving the blanket away from me, I realized that my ankles were still being held by restraints, although my wrists had been freed. Stuck on the bed, I reached my arms out as far as I could without falling off the edge of the mattress and managed to grab hold of the curtain. As I drew it aside, I found myself gazing around at what appeared to be a large hall filled with curtained compartments just like mine. It looked like a hospital ward. And it was quiet. Eerily quiet.

"Hello?" I said, louder this time, my voice echoing off the walls.

No response. I couldn't hear breathing, or signs that there was anybody in this hall except for me.

I'd been so disorientated as to my whereabouts that the obvious question only just dawned on me. *What did they do to me?* I couldn't feel any pain, except for the usual coldness I was accustomed to. Staring down at my body, I realized that I'd been changed. I still wore black, but the material was different. I wore light cotton pajamas. I shuddered. *Who changed me?* I hoped that it had been Jocelyn, or another female hunter.

My eyes scanned the length of my arms, and then I removed my shirt. My chest seemed quite normal. My gaze lowered to my stomach, then to my abdomen... where I froze. There was a faint, thin scar running the width of my lower abdomen. My breath hitched. I leaned forward to get a closer look, running a finger along the mark. As I stared at it, a stronger emotion overtook the horror I felt at what these people had done—or rather, not knowing what they had done.

My fists clenched as anger washed over me in waves.

They couldn't treat me like a lab rat. This couldn't be *legal*.

How dare they do this to me.

Chapter 18: Ben

As I hurtled away from the hunters' lair, I scanned the frosty surroundings. I traveled in the opposite direction from the road I had followed to the ski resort. A few miles behind the cluster of glass buildings was acres of some type of training grounds, cleared of all snow. They were scattered among some of the lower mountains. As I kept speeding and neared what I believed would be the end of the hunters' property, I caught sight of another open field at the foot of an overhanging cliff—about a mile or so away from the training grounds.

Despite the hurry I was in, I couldn't help but pause mid-air and stare.

In the center of the field was a horde of griffins. There

must've been at least fifty, and they appeared much larger and more ferocious than the one I'd seen earlier. Perhaps the latter had been a baby.

The chains that bound these griffins must've been strong to withstand their strength. Then again, there were a lot of strange things about this place—technology that I simply couldn't fathom. Like how they could trap all those supernatural creatures behind glass in the courtyard. It made me wonder if a witch was helping them.

As much as my mind buzzed with questions, I tore my eyes away from the griffins and continued toward the ocean.

I still wasn't sure how I would find my way back to The Shade once I reached the shore. The thought had occurred to me that perhaps the hunters might themselves return to The Shade and resume their mysterious watch over the island. I was not sure what exactly they had been doing observing the island even after our witches had put a stop to their motion sensor technology. Whatever it was, after the incident with the dragons, somehow I doubted that they would be heading back there in a hurry.

My other option would be to find an airport and board a plane bound for Hawaii. Once I reached there, I would have a better chance of locating The Shade. But I did not know where the nearest airport was, or how long it would take me to find it. For now, heading to the ocean seemed like my best bet.

At least I possessed supernatural speed. That was the only advantage I had in this situation.

Arriving at the shore, I touched down on a beach and moved toward the water's edge. I stared out over the expanse of water, trying to get even the slightest bearing. It wasn't a question of if I would get lost; it was a question of when, and for how long.

Grimacing, I was about to lift myself back into the air when my attention was drawn to the sound of scampering behind me. I turned in time to see a giant Great Dane bounding toward me, his owner walking about twenty feet behind him. As he headed excitedly for the waves, the right side of his body brushed through me, and... I felt the strangest sensation.

Warmth.

Heat.

I could *feel* the dog's body as he drifted through me. Others had passed through me before—humans and supernaturals alike—and indeed, I'd caused myself to pass through others, like in the case of Jeramiah after I had discovered his plan to hand my parents over to the hunters. But my encounter with this dog was the first time I had ever *felt* another being's physical body. The feeling had me stunned, mesmerized for a few moments. I'd almost forgotten what the sensation of warmth felt like. I had touched River in dreams, but they were just that—dreams. They weren't real or tangible like the wave of heat sweeping through me caused by the Great Dane.

I was in almost a daze as I stared at the dog, who had reached the edge of the water and was barking loudly to his owner.

I approached the mutt and moved through him deliberately. Again, I felt the heat, the physicality of his body. I bent down, thought overtaking me. *What does this mean?* I needed to continue on my way, but I couldn't help but feel that I'd just made some kind of breakthrough. What exactly, I still didn't know…

I wonder…

An idea sparked in me. I moved toward the animal again. This time, as he stopped jumping about and stood still, sniffing the sand, I stepped through him and stayed there, in his halo of heat. After a few seconds had passed, I suddenly felt an odd suction. As I remained rooted to my spot, I found my ethereal form sinking against—no, down into— the huge dog. As I sank, the heat of its body enveloped me and then my vision became shrouded with blackness… but it was for only a few moments. When the heat of the dog's body fully consumed my spirit, my vision returned.

Only, it was not my vision.

I was seeing through the eyes of the dog.

CHAPTER 19: RIVER

The sight of the scar lining my abdomen caused something to snap in me.

I'm not going to take this anymore. I'm not going to allow them to do this to me!

I didn't know how I would defend myself, and I didn't want to think about what the consequences of that defense would be, but I swore to myself that the next person who tried to touch me would sorely regret it.

Glancing around the empty ward one last time, I grabbed hold of the curtain again and drew it closed around my bed. Then I settled myself on the mattress, placing the blanket over me and repositioning my pillows. I closed my eyes. I didn't know how long it would take for somebody to come and check on me, but I did know that I ought to appear asleep when they arrived. I still had to figure out my game plan, but I felt that it could only work to my advantage if they still thought me to be lost in slumber. So I waited, my eyes clamped tightly shut. I focused on easing my breathing to a slow, steady rate. As I tried to formulate a plan, I glanced at the clock by my bedside every now and then to see how much time was passing. It was early evening now, so it seemed that at least a day had passed since they had operated on me.

As the night progressed, so did my impatience. I began to fidget, the wait becoming agonizing. I had already gone over in my mind a hundred times all the possible things that I could do to try to fight back and escape, but there was only so much I could plan in advance. I just had to wait for someone to come and then play things by ear.

Finally, doors glided open and then closed again. Then the familiar heels clacked against the floor, accompanied by wheels rolling across the floor. I froze, adrenaline beginning to course through my veins.

As she neared my compartment and the sounds of the wheels and heels stopped, my heart skipped a beat. I suddenly became acutely self-conscious about my breathing and the way I was lying. I also realized that my eyes had clamped too tightly shut in my nervousness. I loosened them, trying to force myself to appear relaxed.

The curtain drew aside, and the woman approached my bed. She paused for a moment, and I imagined that she was eyeing my face. Then she touched the blanket that I'd pulled up to my chest. Clasping it, she pulled it down to my feet, then paused again, perhaps now glancing over the rest of my body. She drew in a breath before taking a step back. Metal doors creaked open. There was no metal cupboard by my bed, so I assumed that there must have been a compartment at the base of the trolley she'd wheeled in. She began rummaging through what sounded like pins and plastic containers before standing again and hovering near the edge of my bed.

I picked up on the sound of liquid swishing, and then a kind of suction. I was horribly tempted to open my eyes, but I could not. At least not until…

The woman's hand reached for mine and she raised it at an angle. As another needle made contact with my skin, before it could penetrate deeper than a few millimeters, my eyes shot open. Indeed, it was Jocelyn, wearing her usual lab coat, her mousy hair tied back in a ponytail. Her eyes bulged with alarm. But I didn't give her more than a second to react.

My arms extended, my hands wrapping around her throat and stifling her yelp. Her right hand slipped beneath her coat and fumbled against the outline of a gun, fixed to her belt. Again, I was too quick for her. My strength allowed me to grip her by the neck with one hand while with the other I was free to knock her hand away and snatch up the gun for myself. Noticing a safety catch, I quickly slid it in the opposite direction. Then, gripping the weapon so hard the blood drained from my knuckles, I pointed it at her square in the chest and hissed, "Free my ankles."

Jocelyn's face blanched, her lips quivering. I wasn't even sure what type of bullets this gun was loaded with. I had been shot by one of the hunters' bullets before, back in the desert after escaping from The Oasis. I'd later learned that it had been a special UV bullet, uniquely designed for ending the lives of vampires by burning them up from the inside. The only reason that I hadn't suffered that fate was because I was a half-blood, and their technology didn't have the same effect on me. It had just ended up lodging in my side, but if Ben hadn't come back to help me, I could've easily died from it. Based on the look of fear in Jocelyn's eyes, it was clear that these bullets could do similar damage to humans.

Reaching into her left pocket, she pulled out a set of keys with trembling hands. Then she inched toward the end of my bed. But as she lowered the key to my foot restraints, she stalled.

"I will pull this trigger if I have to," I whispered, pulling my meanest face. "Free me, and don't say a word. If you make a sound or try to call for help, it will be the last call you ever make."

Biting her lip, she nodded. Then she removed the restraints from my ankles, allowing me to swing off the bed and stand on my feet. My knees felt shaky at first, my legs weak—from all the drugs they'd been pumping me with, no doubt—but even as I tried to find my balance, I was careful to hold the gun steadily in front of me.

I moved closer to her and grabbed the collar of her coat with one hand while pressing the gun against her temple with the other.

In that moment, I wasn't sure who was more terrified—Jocelyn or me. Although I'd been forced to use a gun before, during Ben's and my voyage from Egypt to The Shade, I had never been properly taught how to aim. I prayed that I would not have to use this one on Jocelyn. Besides my inexperience, the gunshots would trigger a dozen alarms. And on the subject of alarms, I spotted several CCTV cameras positioned around us on the ceiling—one I was certain was angled enough to spy on my compartment. All it would take would be a casual glance from one of the hunters monitoring the cameras, and a whole horde of them would come rushing into the ward. I pushed Jocelyn roughly against the curtain, where I guessed we'd at least be less visible. But I had to move fast now.

Still careful to keep the gun pressed against her, I whispered against Jocelyn's ear, in a voice barely louder than a breath, "Now, you're going to tell me which of the keys on your chain belongs to your vehicle."

She shook her head in an instant. "I don't own a vehicle."

The keys hung half in, half out of her pocket. I picked them up with one hand and looked them over. One was half covered in thick, black plastic. It so obviously belonged to a vehicle, I was shocked that she had even bothered to lie to me.

I slid the key into the pocket of my pajama shirt, then tightened my grip on her, pressing hard against her larynx.

"Are you telling me this does not belong to a car?"

"It does," she wheezed. "But not my car."

I breathed out in frustration. "I don't care whose car it is. I have the key, and now I want you to take me to it."

"O-Okay. I-It's outside, in the main parking lot."

Outside. Just the thought of stepping outside sent shivers running through me. My pajamas were so thin and my feet were bare. Just standing without my blanket in this ward was already painful enough. I had half a mind to ask Jocelyn to give me her shoes, but she couldn't go roaming around the facility without them. It risked drawing too much attention. I, on the other hand, was looked on as nothing but an animal here, so nobody would give a second glance to my bare feet.

"I'll warn you one last time before we leave," I breathed, my stomach twisting itself into knots as I thought about what I was about to attempt. "Don't dare try to yell, or catch anyone's attention as we pass by. Remember, I have nothing to lose. If I sense that you're leading me in the wrong direction, or if I suspect you're even close to stepping out of line, I will fire a bullet into the base of your spine, which will either kill you or, perhaps worse, paralyze you for life." I glared at her menacingly. "I wouldn't take that risk if I were you."

Jocelyn inhaled a sharp breath before nodding again, apparently having lost her voice.

"If somebody talks to you, you respond casually and end the conversation as soon as possible. You must act normally as we walk, as though you are escorting me somewhere. Stick close to me, and don't try to drift more than half a foot apart. If I sense you drifting further, I'll dig the gun harder against your back as a warning. There will be no second warning."

"A-All right." Jocelyn began moving shakily to step outside of the curtain, but I held her back.

"Wait a moment," I murmured.

We would be in fuller view of the CCTV cameras once we moved out into the main ward area, and before we stepped out, I needed to hide the gun—but not too hidden so that Jocelyn might see me as less of a threat to her life. I eyed the clothes that she was wearing. Beneath her lab coat was a beige cardigan. Roughly pulling off her coat, I tugged on her cardigan. She slipped it off and handed it to me before pulling her coat back on. I bundled the cardigan around my right forearm and pulled it lower down so that it also covered my right hand that held the gun. If I kept my hand close behind her back, even if we passed by someone in the corridors, on cursory glance it should be hard for them to tell that I'd taken Jocelyn hostage—providing she didn't decide to mess things up.

"Okay," I whispered, drawing in a deep breath. "Let's go."

Positioning the gun against her back, I nudged her outside the curtain so that she could lead the way. The two of us exited the compartment and emerged into the vastness of the main ward.

My mind raced and my throat dried out as we moved toward the exit. Assuming we made it to the parking lot, I would have to figure out how to drive. I'd only taken a few driving lessons in my life, before things at home became too hectic and our money ran dry. I hadn't been able to continue learning, and I could only hope that once I sat in the driver's seat, I would remember enough to get by.

The clock had started ticking the moment I threatened Jocelyn. I feared that it wasn't a question of if I would get caught, but when. Even if I managed to control Jocelyn enough to make it to the vehicle, I could not keep control of her forever.

I forced my mind back to the present moment. Jocelyn's pace was too slow for my liking. I gave her a nudge with the gun, which made her speed up. We exited the ward and emerged in a wide corridor outside. She took a right turn until we arrived at a set of elevators. We entered one, and then she punched the number "2". *The second floor.*

I furrowed my brows and my stomach dropped, as I was already feeling suspicious of her. "Why the second floor?" I asked. "I told you that I need you to take me to the parking lot."

"That is the fastest way to the parking lot," she replied in an unsteady whisper. "It's located outside a building a few peaks along from us, and the fastest way to get there is to travel along the walkways."

I relaxed a little. Of course. In all the stress I was under, I'd forgotten that these buildings were perched among a number of different mountain peaks, all interconnected by those terrifyingly transparent walkways.

After exiting the elevator on the second floor, I looked left and right anxiously, thankful that I couldn't spot any hunters walking about. My palm was beginning to feel uncomfortably sweaty against the grip of the gun.

Jocelyn took a left, and we walked to the end of the corridor where, indeed, we arrived at the opening of a walkway. Passing along it, we arrived at another corridor, which eventually led to another walkway. A trio of male hunters were walking along it toward us. I held my breath as they passed, relieved that Jocelyn didn't try anything.

"How much longer?" I whispered, as the hunters disappeared from sight.

"Not much longer," Jocelyn replied in a strained voice.

After what felt like the sixth walkway, I finally spotted the parking lot through the glass walls of the building. I heaved a deep sigh of relief. Although the feeling didn't last long. Even if I managed to figure out how to drive the car away from here, there would surely be some security barriers to get through. I doubted anybody could just drive to and from this place. I realized that I might have no choice but to take

Jocelyn with me, and she would have to give some excuse to the security personnel as to why she needed to drive away with me... And then what? Even if we managed all this, where on earth would I even go? I hadn't the first clue of how to make my way back to The Shade, and I was quite sure that no one on the island knew where I was. They would have noticed that I was missing by now, but they wouldn't have seen me being dragged away by the hunters in their submarine.

Heck, *I* didn't even know where I was.

I shook myself. I had to stop thinking so far ahead and just take this one step at a time. Once I got in the car and got it to start, then I could begin thinking further into the future. At least I would be one step closer to escape than I was an hour ago—however pathetic or small that step might be.

We entered another elevator, and this time, she pressed the button for the ground level. We descended and when the doors glided open, my heart beat faster as I realized that we were going to have to pass through a reception room. Surely there would be more hunters in there. Now more than ever, I needed to keep Jocelyn under my control. As we reached the double doors, which Jocelyn proceeded to march through, I pressed the metal against her back again as a reminder that I meant business.

Moving further into the reception area, I spotted three women sitting behind the wide desk. Each of them looked up from their computer screens at once.

To my angst, the blonde woman spoke up. "All right, Jocelyn?"

I'd been praying that the receptionists wouldn't bother to make conversation. As Jocelyn turned to face the woman, I had to work hard to make my stance look natural as I kept my right hand close to her back.

"Yes, thank you," Jocelyn replied. I winced internally at her uneven voice. I suspected that she was not deliberately trying to give my game away. She was genuinely terrified— as I would be in her position. There probably wasn't much she could do to control her tone. Which meant that this conversation had to end. Now.

From the slight frown on the blonde woman's face, I got the chilling suspicion that she had already caught on that something wasn't quite right. I racked my brain for what I could possibly do to hasten the closure of conversation without making things look even more suspicious.

"Where are you off to with the half-blood?" the woman pressed. My heart palpitated as she stood up from her chair. She began walking toward us.

Oh, God.

I had no choice but to discreetly withdraw my cardigan-clad hand from Jocelyn's back. At least the gun was small, and I was able to raise my right hand to my chest and insert my left hand into the opening of the cardigan—and around the gun—to make it look like I was simply using the garment as a muffler to keep my hands warm.

Jocelyn cleared her throat.

Don't fail me now, Jocelyn.

Please, don't fail me now.

Even though she would be aware now that I had withdrawn the gun from her back, I was still standing behind her, and it would not take much for me to whip it out and fire at her if she took a misstep.

"Just a few tests," Jocelyn replied, her voice thankfully more steady than before.

"Outside?"

"Yes... To experiment with her temperature sensitivity."

"Uh-huh..." The blonde woman's eyes fell on me, glancing briefly at my cardigan-turned-muffler, before she resumed her focus on Jocelyn.

Now go away, nosey woman.

I was ready to let out a sigh of relief when she turned her

back on us. But then her left hand shot beneath her top and when she whirled around to face us again, she was holding a thin silver gun, aimed directly at me.

Chapter 20: River

Christ, these women are prepared. They were like receptionists-cum-security guards. I never would've guessed an innocent-looking receptionist to be hiding a lethal weapon in her cleavage—I guessed their appearance was part of their effectiveness.

I didn't have time to wonder how exactly she had seen through me—maybe they had caught sight of me accosting Jocelyn via the security cameras after all, or perhaps more likely we just looked so darn suspicious. My stupid cardigan-muffler hadn't helped at all. These hunters weren't dumb. They were sharp as knives.

My first instinct was to reach out and grab Jocelyn by the

neck. Pulling her back against me, I whipped out my gun and pressed it against her temple. I held her in front of me like a shield and began pulling her toward the exit.

"Stop where you are!" the blonde hunter yelled.

I ignored her and kept moving backward. Jocelyn whimpered beneath my grasp as I dug the barrel of the gun harder against her skin. Although fear coursed through my veins, I maintained steady eye contact with the gun-wielding receptionist. I had to hope that she valued Jocelyn's life enough to not fire.

I wasn't far from the door now. Perhaps ten feet. From the corner of my eye, I noticed the other receptionists stand up behind the desk. Before any of them could whip out their own guns from their bosoms—or God knew where else they had them stashed—I hissed, "Don't move! I will pull the trigger."

I hurried backward with as much speed as I could without causing Jocelyn to trip. As my back hit against the glass doors, I glanced to my right at the fingerprint scanner. Keeping my gun against Jocelyn with one hand, with the other I reached for her hand and pressed her thumb against the screen.

Come on. Come on!

The doors weren't opening. In fact, the scanner appeared

to be switched off.

Oh no.

I suspected that there must have been a control button for the door behind the desk, and that one of the women had hit it, disabling the exit completely.

I was trapped. And now, perhaps sensing my growing hopelessness, the hunters were becoming more bold. The blonde in front of me began moving closer and the receptionists behind the desk pulled out guns—one had a weapon tucked into the back of her pants, while the other had one stored beneath her shirt like the blonde. Maybe they sensed that I wasn't going to kill Jocelyn. Maybe they thought that I didn't have it in me. I felt desperate enough, but they would be right: I couldn't pull the trigger on Jocelyn. At least, not while the doctor was helpless in my grasp. If she turned around and tried to fight me... that would be another thing.

"Don't come a step closer!" I called, fighting with all that I had to keep my voice steady. I would've shouted, but I didn't want to make any more noise than we already had.

However, my threats were futile. These hunters were obviously highly trained and experienced in high-tension situations, and probably also well educated in psychology. She had already seen through me. She knew I was bluffing.

Either that, or she didn't care much whether or not I shot her colleague.

As the blonde approached within three feet of me, I did the only thing that I could think to do. I thrust Jocelyn forward with such strength that she lost her footing and collided into the hunter. The surprise and force of Jocelyn's movement caused the two of them to go crashing to the floor.

I whirled around to face the exit and fired my gun at the lock that held the glass doors glued together. I figured that this was my best bet, because I was certain that the glass would be bulletproof. The force of the recoil sent shockwaves rippling up my arms. This weapon was powerful for one so small. Thankfully powerful. The lock gave way, and with one strong kick, I was able to force the doors open and thrust myself into the wintry world outside.

The cold hit me like an electric shock. My bare feet sinking into the snow, I wondered how many minutes I could last like this before I developed frostbite. I could not think about it now. I urged my aching limbs forward, faster than I'd ever thought that I could in such conditions. A deafening alarm sounded behind me. I shot a look back over my shoulder to see the receptionists piling out of the door after me, and now they had no doubt summoned God knew how many other hunters to join them in the chase.

It hit me only now that none of them had attempted to fire even a single bullet at me. Not even after I had pushed Jocelyn away from me and turned my back to face the glass doors. I had been fast, but these hunters weren't exactly lacking in their reflexes. One of the hunters behind the desk could have at least attempted to hit me if she had wanted to. I could only conclude that I really was of value to them. They didn't want to kill me, not even after what I had done to Jocelyn. They wanted only to recapture me.

This might have been my one advantage. I could run without the constant need to dodge bullets. *Although, on second thoughts, they might attempt to hit me with some kind of sedative-tinged bullet to bring me down...*

Still clutching Jocelyn's gun in my hand, I darted into the midst of the parking lot, ducking beneath vehicles as I sped forward, trying to remain out of sight as much as I could.

I heard more shouting—the voices of men this time. More hunters had arrived already, but this time I didn't look back. The sight of dozens of hunters piling out of the entrance would only increase my panic and inability to think clearly.

Heavy snowflakes started to fall, impairing my vision as I tried to make out the parking lot's exit. It was difficult enough as it was because I had to keep ducking out of sight, fearful to remain exposed for more than a few seconds at a time.

And then I spotted it—a gate. While the rest of the massive parking lot was enclosed by a high and, by the looks of it, electrified fence, the gate looked like something one might see in a supermarket parking lot. It was more of a barrier than a gate. Something that wouldn't be difficult for me to climb over. A surge of hopefulness running through me, I abandoned caution and hurtled toward the barrier for dear life.

I stopped dead in my tracks about ten feet away.

Three male hunters in ski jackets and heavy boots emerged from the small cubicle near the barrier. They had already been warned. They were expecting me.

I darted sideways, plunging beneath a large truck. Scrambling along its underbelly, I emerged on the other side of it, now forced to take a different direction. I gazed around at the high fence. It was humming with electricity, and its top was spiked with barbed wire. Even with my strength and speed, how would I ever escape over that without either being electrocuted to a crisp or mangled by the barbs?

Hunters' footsteps trudged through the snow a short distance away. I kept moving, sliding beneath vehicles and winding in and out of the parking spaces until I reached the very edge of the enclosure. There was a large SUV parked right next to the fence. I crawled beneath it and paused to catch my breath.

But it had been a mistake to stop moving. No longer distracted by the swift movement of my limbs, I became fully aware of just how much trauma the freezing temperature was causing my body. As I crouched down in the snow, clad in icy wet pajamas and half submerged in snow, I had lost all feeling in my hands, feet and face. And I could feel the numbness spreading—up along my legs, and arms. My throat was tight, my chest restricted, and it was a struggle to even breathe. As I shivered, it was from the very core of me.

Can half-bloods die of hypothermia?

I can't sit here and wait to find out.

I have to keep moving.

I have to keep moving.

My brain addled with panic, I barely even thought about what I was doing as I left my hiding place and staggered out into the open.

Gazing around the parking lot through the thickening snowfall, I expected dozens of hunters to spot me at once and begin racing in my direction.

Instead, every hunter I laid eyes on had their gaze fixed on the sky, an expression of shock on their face.

"How did it escape?" one of the hunters bellowed. It sounded like Mark.

Although these hunters certainly treated me like an object, based on where they were all looking, I was pretty sure that by *it,* he wasn't referring to me.

An explosion of gunshots pierced the frigid atmosphere.

I craned my neck upward in the direction where they were staring and shooting toward to try to make out what exactly had caught their attention. So much so that they seemed to have temporarily forgotten about me.

It didn't take long for me to spot "it".

I could barely believe my eyes as I gazed up at the snow-speckled sky. A giant monster with the head, wings and sharp talons of a fearsome bird; the body, tail and hind legs of a lion. It was holding a hunter in its deadly grasp.

I must be hallucinating.

Maybe I'm still lying beneath that SUV.

Maybe this is what happens to a person dying of cold.

And yet, by now, I'd seen enough strange things in the world. I had no idea where on earth it had come from, but why shouldn't I believe my eyes? Why shouldn't I believe in a half-lion, half-bird creature, when I myself was half-vampire, half-human? Now it occurred to me that its characteristics were identical to that of a griffin— a supernatural creature I'd read about when studying mythology at school.

A piercing screech emanated from the griffin's mouth, snapping me out of my daze.

What am I doing?

The hunters are distracted.

There's nobody guarding the exit.

Once again trying to keep my head down low beneath the vehicles in case any of the hunters decided to chase me even in the midst of this beast's presence, I hurtled once again toward the exit.

This time, I reached it. Heck, I even leaped over the barrier and landed on the other side. Before me was a long, snow-covered road that appeared to wind down through the mountains. I had to force myself to run fast again, even though my bones ached and creaked. Not only did I have to lose sight of the hunters, I also had to maintain what little energy I had left in me.

Leaving the road—for that was far too obvious a place to run—I began racing toward the cluster of nearby rocks at the foot of one of the mountain slopes. I figured that I ought to go off track as far as possible, even if I did end up getting lost—being lost was better than falling back into the hands of the hunters. Anything felt better than that. Even running barefoot in sodden pajamas through a snowstorm.

I had just reached the start of the slope when I heard another round of gunshots, followed by more shouting, the crunching of footsteps through snow… and then the heavy beating of wings, close to me. Too close.

I whirled around to the terrifying sight of the griffin hurtling directly toward me. It soared over the barrier with supernatural speed and caught up with me within a matter of seconds. I barely even had a chance to recover from the shock and attempt to run for shelter before it had reached me.

Now that it was so close, I realized just how large it was. Not quite the size of a dragon, but not that far off, either.

Its talons extended and closed around my shoulders. I cried out, certain it was on the verge of taking a bite out of me. Instead, the griffin's wings beat hard and I found myself being hoisted into the air. It ascended quickly in the sky, so quickly that I barely even had a chance to consider whether I ought to attempt to wriggle free and leap back down to the ground, before the jump became too scary for me to even consider it.

Casting my eyes down on the parking lot, I took in the number of hunters down there for the first time. There must've been at least fifty of them—most of them now close to the gate where they had no doubt run after me—their guns still raised in the air. They had stopped firing by now, perhaps realizing that we were too far away. Or perhaps even now, they didn't want to risk shooting me.

As the griffin ascended still higher with me, the hunters became nothing but specks of dirt on a blanket of snow, and soon, even the buildings and the mountain peaks became miniature. I couldn't bear to look down any longer. I could only be thankful that the creature was holding me firmly.

In an attempt to distract myself from the height, I craned my neck upward and looked over the griffin with a mixture of trepidation and fascination. I realized that it was a male, and I noticed a bloody wound—two in fact—in the side of him where the hunters no doubt had managed to shoot him. Clearly the bullets hadn't penetrated deep enough to be fatal. Either that, or the beast was impervious to the bullets.

For the first time, I became aware of how much heat the griffin's body was radiating. He was holding me close to him, and my back touched the swell of his chest. He must have been hot blooded, and being so huge helped. Even as the harsh wind howled around me, and despite my absurd position, the warmth of this creature began to feel almost comforting.

I gazed up at the griffin's face.

Where did he come from? And why is he rescuing me?

I realized with a shudder that I should not be too quick in assuming that this creature was rescuing me. Maybe he had been flying by, and simply saw me as an easy dinner.

I averted my eyes to his solid talons wrapped around me, his warmth suddenly becoming less appealing.

I ought not get too cuddly with him yet.

CHAPTER 21: RIVER

I remained tense for what felt like the next half hour—or perhaps it was a full hour—as the griffin continued to fly high in the sky. By now, we must have created miles and miles of distance between us and the hunters' facility.

Then, with a sudden billowing of his wings, we slowed and began to descend. I dared look down at the ground, but then averted my gaze again as the griffin launched into a dive that was almost as fast and terrifying as a freefall. I clamped my eyes shut and kept them closed until I felt a shudder. I cautiously lifted my eyelids to see that we had landed outside a cave. A cave etched into the side of a towering snowy mountain.

He's brought me back to his lair.

He's going to eat me.

The griffin's talons loosened around me and I leapt to the ground. My feet crushing against sharp rocks, I began to run in the opposite direction of the cave. I winced as the snow once again numbed my bare feet, but I didn't have to endure it for long. The griffin caught up and whipped in front of me with alarming speed, blocking my way. I staggered back, gazing up at the creature's face. Although it was fierce, strangely, there was something calm, almost reassuring about his demeanor as he looked me steadily in the eye. I should have been terrified for my life, but even as he stood, blocking my way, I couldn't bring myself to feel much more than confusion and curiosity. *What is the deal with this beast?* I frowned, cocking my head to one side.

He began moving forward, and, nudging the top of his smooth, orange beak against my belly, herded me back toward the cave. I tried to circle around him, but again, he was quick to cut me off before I could.

I threw a glance over my shoulder into the cave. I guessed at least it would be warmer in there. *But why does he want me there?*

If he had been intending to eat me, why would he wait for me to walk into the cave? He was a monster. He could rip me in two with a chomp of his beak. He didn't need me in the cave to do that, and heck, even if he did, he could carry me there himself.

I glanced from the cave, to the deserted, icy landscape surrounding us, then back to the cave. It didn't seem that I had any choice but to obey the griffin's whims. He wasn't letting me leave, and I was positive that if I did somehow skirt around him and hurtle down the mountainside, he would only launch into the sky and scoop me up again.

So I turned to face the cave. The tip of his beak nudged against my back as he ushered me inside. Once I had neared the back of the cavern, winding around the stalagmites, I stopped and turned around again to face the creature. Planting my hands on my hips, I raised a brow as if to ask him, *Now what?*

To my shock, I could've sworn that he actually nodded. He gestured with his head toward one of the large, flat rocks at the back of the cave, as if... telling me to sit down?

Cautiously, I moved to the rock he'd indicated, and sat.

"What are you?" I whispered, my nose scrunching in confusion.

The creature stared at me, his beady brown eyes deep and soulful.

Can he really understand what I'm saying?

I couldn't shake the feeling that he understood me. There was something so… sentient about his eyes.

"What do you want with me?" I whispered.

He glanced toward the exit, and then looked up at the sky—which was now darkening. What was he trying to tell me? It looked like he was indicating that he wanted to fly away with me, but hadn't he just done that? Why bring me to the cave?

"You want to take me outside?" I asked.

Again, he nodded.

"Where?"

He expelled a caw, and I sensed frustration in his eyes. He threw his head back over his shoulder again, to indicate outside.

I stood up and began to head toward the exit. Again, he caught up with me, and ushered me back to the rock.

Now it was my turn to breathe out in frustration.

I didn't understand him. If he wanted to take me outside, why did he bring me to this cave in the first place and why was he insisting that I sit on this rock? I frowned. "I don't belong here," I said, speaking slowly and careful to enunciate each syllable. "I need to go home."

I heaved a sigh. At least this cave was warm with the griffin in it. His body emanated heat like a radiator.

He backed away from me, and sat down a few feet away. As the minutes passed, his warmth eased the pain in my aching bones and loosened my tight muscles, making me feel relaxed. He averted his attention away from me and gazed out at the dark, frozen world outside.

He made no motion to stand up again, and I found myself trapped at the back of the cave. It looked like he was keeping watch… perhaps even guarding me. Clearly, I was going to need to wait for him to fall asleep before I could attempt to escape.

For now, I might as well rest my traumatized body. I didn't know when the next opportunity to do so would crop up.

I curled up on the rock, and even though it was hard and bumpy, I felt more comfortable than I ever had in the hunters' soft bed.

Many hours must've passed as I lay there, eyeing the creature and waiting for him to nod off. But he didn't.

What he did do, however, as he kept watch over the cave throughout the night, was glance back at me every five minutes with what I could've sworn was a look of concern in his eyes.

Chapter 22: Ben

I remained close to River until she fell asleep. I knew that she would eventually. The trauma that she must've been through would have drained her, and she needed to recuperate.

Then, in the very early hours of the morning, I dared move to the exit of the cave and launch into the sky. I hated to leave her, but it would be only for a short while. We had a long journey ahead of us, and I wanted to do all I could to make sure that it would be as painless for her as possible.

As I beat the griffin's wings and lifted silently in the air, my mind returned to all that had passed since I'd discovered that I could possess the body of an animal.

I didn't know how it was possible, but after I'd seeped into the body of the Great Dane and found myself seeing through his eyes, I soon realized that I could also control his movements. His legs became like my own, my will his will.

I was certain that I wasn't able to possess human beings or other supernaturals with the same level of consciousness. It made me speculate that perhaps ghosts could possess animals because animals' awareness wasn't as high as the former. Maybe, since their minds were less developed, there was less resistance and they were easier to control. Whatever the reason, I had made a breakthrough. I could inhabit animals.

After making this discovery thanks to the dog, all my plans changed. I was no longer going to head back to The Shade. That had been the last thing I'd wanted to do in any case. It would've taken a long time to find and I'd resorted to it solely out of lack of any other plan. But now... now I had another plan. What would hopefully be a better, faster plan.

I drifted out of the dog's body on the beach, relinquishing control. The animal let out a snort before moving back toward his owner with shaky legs, as though recovering from the shock and confusion of my possession.

Then I headed right back to the hunters' lair. As I sped through the sky, I tried to formulate a plan in my mind. The first thing I wanted to do was verify River's whereabouts—

that she was still in the same place as before. I had been heading toward the courtyard, but as I passed the main reception area near the parking lot, I spotted her there, standing behind a woman in a lab coat and facing the reception desk. I remained observing the scene, wondering what River's game plan was, but then a blonde hunter pulled out a gun, and I didn't have another moment to lose. As much as it killed me to leave River, I immediately sped away.

Prior to spotting River in the reception, my hurriedly cobbled-together plan had been to see if there were any domestic animals roaming the building that I could possess. Perhaps pets of the hunters. If I found one, I could enter the animal and find a way to roam the building in search of Mark—whom I assumed would have a key. Now this was all out of the question. There was no time.

As I racked my brain as to what I could possibly do after this turn of events, my mind suddenly trailed back to the griffins I'd spotted, tethered in an open field some miles away from the main facility. I headed there immediately.

On arriving, before trying to figure out how I was going to let one of them free, I first had to verify that I could indeed inhabit these creatures. I dipped down and touched the nearest one to me—a male. Sure enough, I found myself sinking into him, just as I had done to the dog, and a few seconds later the griffin's eyes were my eyes. I could move his limbs at my will. I glanced down at the chains that bound his feet and noticed a sturdy padlock holding them in place. I needed the key.

I left the griffin—who reacted in a similar way to the dog had, snorting and looking irritable and disorientated—and turned my focus on the nearby cabin. Through the window, I spied two male hunters sitting inside it. When I hurried toward the cubicle, its door was slightly ajar. I seeped through it and emerged on the inside. Close to the hunters now, I decided to double-check my assumption that I definitely couldn't inhabit humans. I moved toward him and tried to step into his being, but, as I had expected, I only passed through him. He wasn't receptive to my spirit.

Stepping back, I glanced around the cabin—surprisingly large on the inside. My eyes fell on a dog in one corner of the room. A large pitbull terrier. He was curled up on a cushion, snoozing. He was a guard dog, no doubt, and perhaps he even helped in some way with the griffins.

My eyes continued raking over the room in search of a set of keys. I spotted them looped on a chain that was attached to the belt of one of the hunters.

Good.

I moved toward the dog, and although he was much

smaller than the Great Dane, as I planted my wispy feet through his back, I was able to inhabit him with relative ease. I felt almost a slight suction, and I began sinking downward, like I'd trodden on quicksand. And the next thing I knew, I was sharing the pitbull terrier's gaze. I stood up, and, after taking a few seconds to get used to walking in his body, padded over to the hunter with the keys. I growled and nuzzled my head against his leg.

"What is it, boy?" he asked, reaching a hand down to scratch my right ear.

I eyed the keys. It wouldn't be hard to rip them from his pants, not with this set of jaws. But then I would need to make it to the field and actually open the chains—all before they caught up with me and punished the dog for my misbehavior.

I let out a low, contented growl, and began licking the hand of the hunter who was still petting me. Even as panic still flooded my mind over River's plight, I couldn't help but feel overwhelmed by the bizarreness of the situation.

So this is what it's like to be a dog.

My life right now—if one could even call it that—was crazier than a dream. *Or should I say a nightmare?*

I nudged my head toward the keys, groaning as though I was enjoying the hunter's attention, and then, once I was close enough, I clamped the dog's jaws firmly around them and tugged hard. The hunter yelped, but before he could grab hold of me, I raced to the door. Slamming my head against it to force it open further, I squeezed the dog's muscled body out of it and began bounding across the snow toward the field.

As I approached, several of the griffins noticed me. They began screeching, flapping their wings and extending their lethal talons in the dog's—my—direction. Their powerful bodies kicked up a storm of snow around them.

Dammit.

Still clutching the metal keychain tightly between my teeth, I was forced to slow down and circle around them. As it turned out, the violent flailing of all their wings at once became a blessing in disguise. The flurry of feathers and the flying of snow made it harder for the hunters to spot me. It also impaired the vision of the griffins themselves, and by the time they had calmed down, I'd managed to approach one of the creatures from behind. The same one I'd just possessed. His head was turned in the other direction, and he apparently hadn't noticed me yet. I needed to keep it that way.

An unpleasant high-pitched sound assaulted my eardrums. A dog whistle, I guessed. Well, I was no dog and

the hunters' antics would not work on me.

I crawled slowly between the griffin's back legs and crept along beneath his sleek underbelly. As I neared the lock that held the chains in place, I was faced with yet another challenge.

How does a dog unlock a padlock?

I couldn't use my feet. They were too clumsy. I had no choice but to use my jaws.

At least it was clear to me which of the keys would fit the padlock—the largest one. The rest were obviously too small. But I needed this large key to jut out from my mouth so that I could push it into the lock and twist it at the right angle. The seconds that followed were tense as I fought to adjust the keys between my teeth, using my tongue as an anchor, all the while trying not to make a sound. Finally, I managed it. The largest key protruding from between my front teeth, I crept toward the padlock, jammed the key into the lock and yanked my head sharply to one side. To my relief, there was a soft click. I kept twisting the key until the padlock opened.

I'd freed the griffin. Now, he just needed to realize it.

Discarding the keys in the snow, I barked. As the griffin's head shot downward, I raced away between his legs. And then I left the dog's body. I didn't want to be responsible for the canine being ripped to pieces—he'd likely be too disorientated after my possession to escape the beast—so I hurried back to the griffin and sank myself into him.

After fifteen tense seconds of trying to figure out how to work his wings, I managed to launch into the sky. The hunters yelled from the ground, but it was too late. I gained speed and soon they became small dots on the white ground.

I soared back to where I had left River, relieved that the creature possessed supernatural speed.

By the time I arrived, River had already managed to break out of the reception somehow, and several dozen hunters were searching the parking lot for her. I strained my eyes to spot River. I couldn't. I moved closer to the ground, deciding that wherever she was, creating a distraction for her would help. I'd approached with great stealth, and the hunters hadn't even noticed me... yet. Trailing my eyes on the ground, I singled out a hunter who looked particularly alone and swooped down toward him. By the time he realized what was happening, I'd already caught him between the griffin's talons and begun crushing his limbs. His yells caught the attention of all the hunters. Several of them fired bullets at me. As I raced higher again, a couple of them lodged painfully into my side, but although they hurt like hell, they didn't hamper my flight. They didn't seem to affect me much more than a bee sting. I'd caught them off guard, and they apparently weren't equipped with strong enough weaponry to take down a griffin.

Then I spotted River, racing over the barrier, in soaking wet pajamas, toward the foot of the nearest mountain. Discarding the hunter unceremoniously and sending him hurtling down into the crowd of hunters gathered beneath me, I shot toward River and managed to scoop her up. I'd been afraid that I would hurt her with my talons, but I didn't have a choice. From the terror in her eyes as she first laid eyes on me, she certainly wasn't going to voluntarily leap onto my back.

I flew with her until I found a cave, where I wanted her to rest for the night.

And now… now, in these early morning hours, I needed to prepare for the journey ahead of us. There were three things I needed to scout for River: warm clothes, food and water.

I was still faced with the same obstacle as before when I'd planned to return to The Shade in my ghostly form: I didn't know exactly how to reach it. I had to be prepared for delays.

Flying over the mountains, I headed back to the ski resort I'd found earlier. I was guessing that they would have a shop filled with ski suits and thermal clothing that would be perfectly suited to River. I was right—there was a ski shop around the back of the resort, in its own designated building. With a thrust of my sharp beak, I broke through one of the wide glass windows, setting off a loud alarm in the process. But it didn't matter. I would be quick.

I lunged for a rail of puffer coats. Trying not to cause any tears, I flung one over my shoulder and caught it with my tail, where it hung by the hood. Next, I collected thermal trousers, socks, boots, as well as a sturdy bag, scooping them up in my talons.

Once I was finished in the clothing section, to my pleasant surprise, I spotted a shelf filled with hiking supplies and long-life food. I added packets of protein bars to the contents in my talons, and then some bottles of water, until I could hold no more.

By the time security guards were racing from the main building toward the shop, I'd already launched back into the sky and flown off with the goods.

River was still asleep when I touched down outside the cave. The cavern had become chilly again without the heat of the griffin's large body. After emptying my talons of the bag, packaged food and water, I crept over to River. I rested the coat gently over her like a blanket, and placed the other clothing items near where she rested. Then I retook my place several feet away from her.

River stirred slightly, clutching the coat more tightly against her. The expression of peace that overtook her face as she settled and lost herself in deep slumber again warmed my spirit more than the griffin's body ever could.

Chapter 23: River

As I opened my eyes to a cave flooded with sunlight, I cursed myself for having fallen asleep. I'd meant to stay up all night and watch for my opportunity to escape from this oddly possessive creature. Now, I might need to wait another day.

Sitting up, I realized that a coat had been resting over me. It was a ski-coat, apparently brand new, with its label still attached. Perched on another rock a few feet away from me was a pair of padded ski pants, warm boots and high thermal socks. Frowning, I gazed toward the exit. The griffin was standing there, close to the ledge, and gazing out at the snowy landscape, like a king beholding his kingdom.

Could he have found these clothes for me?

Rubbing the sleep from my eyes, I slid off the rock. My torn pajamas were bone dry—it must have been the effect of the griffin's body heat all night. With the rays of sun streaming in through the entrance of the cave, I felt almost comfortable. I was still confused by the mysterious appearance of the ski garments, but however they'd gotten here, I wasn't going to look a gift horse in the mouth.

Wrapping the jacket around me and pulling up the zipper to my chin, I slid into the cozy pants before putting on the socks and boots. Then I moved through the cave and cautiously approached the griffin. Next to him was a large bag filled with... energy bars? And bottled water? *Did this creature really find these for me, too?*

Sensing my approach, the griffin turned around and gazed down at me. I furrowed my brows, gesturing to my clothes and the food. "Did you get these for me?"

He nodded.

My eyes widened, and I was rendered speechless. I wondered where he'd found them... and yet again I found myself wondering, *Why would he do this for me?*

"Thank you," I said, taken aback, yet immensely grateful at the same time.

I was feeling starved. I stooped down and scooped up one of the bars, unwrapping it and finishing it within a few mouthfuls. As bland as it tasted, I couldn't deny it was filling. Cracking open one of the bottles and taking a swig of water, I cleared my throat, unsure of what to do or say next. I looked out at the snowcapped landscape, admiring its beauty as it shimmered in the morning sun. I wondered what time it was. But most of all I wondered, *What now?*

I turned my focus back on the griffin.

"I need to leave," I said, still feeling slightly crazy to be having a one-way conversation with an animal. "I live on an island known as The Shade. I need to return there."

The moment I mentioned the island, he began nodding vigorously. I paused, my mouth agape. "You... You know about The Shade?"

Again he nodded.

Perhaps I ought not be so surprised. The Shade was well-known among supernatural creatures, both in the human realm as well as in the supernatural dimension. I just hadn't expected this... thing to be so cognizant.

Then a thought struck me. *What if this griffin has been sent from The Shade to rescue me? Maybe he's an ally, and they sent him to find me. What other explanation could there possibly be for his not only rescuing me, but also looking after me so well?*

Within an instant, I warmed to the beast.

"Were you sent by someone in The Shade?"

At this, he paused and tilted his head to the side, as if he was perhaps unsure of my question or how to answer.

"Do you know where The Shade is?"

He nodded again.

"Will you take me there?"

He screeched, still moving his head up and down. He threw his head over his shoulder, as if indicating to the world outside. And then his legs folded beneath him and he sank to the ground. His gaze was expectant. He had lowered himself for me to climb onto his back.

Still gaping at him, barely daring to believe that I was understanding the situation rightly, I snatched up the bag of supplies from the ground and, tightening my coat around me, swung onto his back. Planting my legs on either side of him, I placed the bag between my thighs.

Is he really going to take me home?

Home. It was strange that I called The Shade my home when I had hardly spent any time there. And yet it felt more like home than New York ever had.

The griffin's wings beat, and he launched into the air. With the heat of his body flowing into me, as well as the ski clothes I was wearing, I felt shielded from the cold. The garments seemed to be of high quality, and once I pulled the hood over my head to protect my ears and the sides of my face, even the wind didn't bother me much.

I gripped the back of his neck tighter as we flew faster. The hunters' facility was in view. Though I was curious to see more of that place from a bird's-eye perspective, I still felt so traumatized by the experience that I'd had there—what they'd done to me, what I feared they might have taken from me—that I preferred to keep my eyes straight ahead and ignore their sprawling lair of horrors.

Then I caught sight of the ocean in the distance. I didn't know how long it would take us to reach The Shade, or how many thousands of miles we were away from it, but as we arrived at the shoreline and launched over the glistening waves, I didn't feel far away from it any more. I had faith in this griffin—my unexpected savior and protector—and I trusted that it was only a matter of time before I was reunited with my family... *And maybe, just maybe, Ben might have returned home in my absence.*

Patting the side of the griffin's head fondly, I couldn't help but whisper, "Thank you."

Chapter 24: River

The journey didn't go as smoothly as I'd hoped. As we soared over the waves with supernatural speed, I got a hunch that the griffin didn't know exactly where he was going after all. He seemed to fly God knew how many miles in one direction, only to turn back on himself and zig-zag in the other. I could only hope that the ocean beneath us was indeed the Pacific Ocean, for I didn't even know for sure where the hunters' lair had been located.

As the hours turned into days, I became increasingly grateful that the creature had thought to procure some food and water for me for the journey, and my only hope that we were headed at least roughly in the right direction came from the increasingly mild temperature. With the heat of the griffin's body seeping into me, combined with my heavy-duty clothing and the sun overhead, I found myself sweating like a pig and I had to discard the ski clothes in favor of my pajamas alone.

"How much longer?" I wondered out loud several times during our flight, even though I knew my companion couldn't answer. He only grunted.

By the third day, I'd finished all the energy bars, but thankfully not all the drinking water. As a half-blood, it was lucky that I didn't need to consume as much and I seemed to be able to bear hunger better than a human.

My impatience and worry satiated a little when I finally spied an island in the distance. A small one. But amidst the endless water, it was a welcome sight.

Then, half a day later, a larger landmass loomed on the horizon. A much larger landmass. *Could this be... Hawaii?* I hardly dared even hope for it, yet it looked like it could be. Moving closer to the shore, I could better make out the island—a landscape of rugged cliffs and golden beaches. As we continued to fly around its border, I began to notice more developed areas, marked by winding roads and towering skyscrapers.

My escort seemed to sense my rising excitement. He let

out a shriek, and nodded enthusiastically toward the island. I guessed that was a good sign.

We continued past the landmass, and even as we were once again engulfed in a world of infinite, rippling blue, my anticipation increased.

By the time night fell, even though the griffin still appeared to get disorientated at times, I couldn't shake the feeling that we were close. Very close.

And then, in what I guessed must have been the early hours of the morning, with a lurch of my heart, I spotted a familiar cluster of rocks. I was sure that they were the same rocks I'd headed to with the dragons to save Sofia, Derek and Aiden.

Oh, my God.

We've arrived.

We've arrived!

"You did it, Hero!" I positively squealed, surprising myself.

Hero. I wasn't sure where that came from. He ought to have a name, and Hero seemed like an appropriate one.

I squeezed my legs more tightly on either side of his back, excitement and relief flooding my brain. I could hardly believe it. I threw a glance over my shoulder toward where the hunters had been positioned in their huge naval ships.

All the ships were gone now. Perhaps they'd all left soon after I'd been taken away in the submarine. Maybe after the incident with the dragons, they'd thought it best to abandon their posts for a while.

I threw my gaze back toward the direction of the invisible island.

"Yes! Over there!" I breathed, pointing toward where I remembered the boundary being in relation to the small rock formation. Of course, it wasn't like I needed to point. Even if Hero had gotten a bit lost during the journey, he'd managed to find his way here in the end across the vast Pacific Ocean.

He hurtled full speed toward the boundary, and just as I was sure that we'd reach it any second, he halted midair with such force, it was like he'd just hit a brick wall. My grip on him loosened and I almost went tumbling down into the waves.

My heart sank a little in my chest. He wasn't able to enter the barrier.

But why not? I was accompanying him. *Don't I still have permission to enter the island?*

I drew in a deep breath. It wasn't the end of the world. We just had to fly around the boundary and make enough noise until somebody noticed and came to collect us.

This idea seemed to occur to my trusty guardian before I even suggested it. Quickly recovering from the sudden stop, he launched us high into the sky—high enough to begin soaring over the island itself. He dipped down occasionally, as if testing the magical boundary that covered the island like a canopy.

"Hello!" I began to bellow as loudly as I could. "It's River! Let me in!"

Since it was early morning, I guessed that many would be asleep, but the island was filled with supernatural creatures with supernatural hearing and I doubted that it would take long for somebody to notice me and come to my aid. Besides, many of them didn't sleep regular hours anyway, since it was always night in The Shade.

"River!"

I froze as a voice called out from beneath us.

It was a male voice, with a thick, Scottish accent.

"I see you through the boundary, River!" the voice called up to us again. "This is Cameron!"

"Oh! Thank you!" I yelled back down. I barely knew Cameron. I had met him and his family only briefly.

"Stay where you are," he ordered. "I'm going to send a witch up for you."

"Thank you!" I replied, and then all was quiet again.

Hero didn't seem to require me to instruct him to stay put. He had heard Cameron, and he paused mid-air, his wings keeping us hovering in one spot.

We were waiting perhaps twenty minutes before Corrine manifested before us out of thin air. She beamed at me, her expression filled with relief, and then her eyes fell on Hero.

"Thank you so much for sending him!" I said. "I dread to think what might have happened to me if he'd arrived even a bit later…"

The witch frowned, her face twisting in bewilderment. "Wait… What? Who's *he?*"

I faltered, staring at Corrine.

"This… creature," I said slowly, patting the back of Hero's smooth head.

Corrine raised a brow. "Honey, I'm relieved as heck to have you back, but I've no idea what you're talking about…" She moved closer to us, her eyes bulging with a mixture of confusion and fascination. "What are you doing with a griffin?"

I felt lost for words. "Are you sure that nobody in The Shade sent him to come and save me?"

"I'm positive," Corrine said, her tone slightly high-pitched as she examined the creature. "I came searching for you myself soon after you were kidnapped, but I failed to find you on any of the hunters' ships. None of us have had a clue where to look for you."

My gaze tilted to Hero, who, except for his wings, was quite still, his eyes bright and receptive. "Then where did he come from?" I breathed.

"You're asking me?" Corrine exclaimed. She tore her eyes away from Hero and fixed them back on me. "Are you all right? What happened to you?"

"I'm okay... I think. The hunters took me back to some kind of headquarters surrounded by mountains and snow. I'll tell you everything, but I just need to see my family first."

"Of course," she said. She approached me and held out her hand for me to take. I assumed that if I grabbed hold of it, I would hover with her too, but...

"Hero," I said. When Corrine's eyes widened, I clarified, "That's my name for him. I, uh, I'd like to bring him down too. I owe him my life, and I feel guilty just leaving him up here. Even if he doesn't stay on the island, we've been traveling for days and I'd like to see if he'll accept some food and water."

Corrine dared reach out a hand and placed it against Hero's sleek neck, as if testing to see if he would snap at her. Strangely, Hero flinched a little at her touch, but then he became still again.

"He's been nothing but gentle with me," I assured her. "I'm sure he's of no threat to anyone."

"Hm," Corrine muttered. "A lot of things have changed in The Shade since you left. We've instituted higher levels of security than we've ever had before. The island has become like a fortress—not even the residents have permission to enter as they please any more. Once out of The Shade, you're stuck out. As inconvenient as it is, there are only three people with the ability to let you in—currently the three most powerful witches of The Shade: myself, Ibrahim or Shayla."

She moved her hand against mine, and to my surprise, I felt a strange prickle run along my arm. Like a mild electric shock. Then Corrine moved backward, and nodded. "What I just did was verify that you're really River and not some imposter disguised by a spell. I must do this with any resident who leaves the island and returns, though admittedly, we've had a lot fewer people wandering off outside of late what with all this hunter craziness…"

"But will you allow me to bring Hero down?"

She nodded, to my relief. "I tested him just now. He's under no disguise. He is… actually a griffin. I guess our island is already a zoo. An extra supernatural shouldn't make a lot of difference to anyone. Let's go down."

I wasn't expecting Corrine to climb onto Hero's back, but

she did, settling behind me. Again, Hero's intuition was uncannily sharp and he didn't wait for either of us to urge him down. He took a dive, and Corrine's arms slid around my waist and tightened, while I gripped his neck. With Corrine making contact with the both of us, we were able to pass through the boundary and then... *Oh, sweet relief.* I gazed down at the most welcome sight. The magical island couldn't have looked more beautiful to me than it did in that moment, as we soared over its sea of redwood trees, its picturesque mountains looming in the distance.

Being back here, in Ben's home, filled me with an unbearable surge of longing for him. Although I was almost certain Corrine's answer would disappoint me, I couldn't stop myself from asking, "Has he returned?"

I'd been so absorbed in thinking about Ben... my love, my best friend... that I didn't even refer to him by his name. But Corrine understood.

"He hasn't," she responded quietly. "I'm sorry."

I swallowed hard, hollowness welling in the pit of my stomach.

There was a span of silence before Corrine spoke again. "So you, uh, want to see your family first, yes?"

"Yes," I replied, my voice lower than usual.

"That's a good idea," Corrine said, in a painfully obvious

attempt to keep the subject on other matters. "Your mom has been worried sick." She pointed toward a clearing in the trees beneath us. "The Vale is down there, if you want to descend with… what did you call him?"

I smirked. "Hero."

"Hero. Well, if you're certain he's safe, he can fly down there with you to the town and you can go see your family. In the meantime, I'd like to inform everyone else that you've returned." She slid off the griffin's back and soared in the air alongside us. She gave me a warm smile and squeezed my hand. "Your mom and siblings aren't the only ones on this island who've been worried about you."

I returned her smile. "Thank you," I said.

With that, Corrine vanished, leaving me and my trusty escort alone again. He had already begun descending toward the clearing. We leveled with the tops of the trees, and the Vale's town square appeared directly beneath us. As he landed gracefully near one of the fountains, I slipped off his back. My knees felt unsteady after being seated for so long, and it took a moment for me to find my balance. Then I faced the griffin, looking him directly in the eye. Slowly, I leaned forward and planted a kiss on the side of his face.

"Thank you," I whispered, meaning it from the very core

of me.

He nudged my shoulder, as if urging me to go see my family.

"Wait here," I said, still having no idea whether this creature would want to stay in The Shade after I'd fed him, or where else he might go if he left. "I'll come back for you very soon."

Turning, I cast one last glance over my shoulder before I bolted toward the street where our townhouse was situated. I was oddly short of breath as I reached the door and knocked. It took three minutes for somebody to wake up. I caught the sound of a door groaning open upstairs, and then footsteps padding down the staircase. It was Jamil who answered the door. His jaw dropped open as he laid eyes on me.

"River!"

I leapt into his arms and hugged him tight.

"Mom!" he bellowed over his shoulder. "River's back!"

Doors burst open upstairs, and my mom and two sisters came stampeding down the staircase. They squealed and threw themselves at me, holding me so close I found it a struggle to breathe.

I returned their affection, kissing and hugging each of them.

"Are you okay? What in heaven's name happened to you, girl?" my mom cried, clutching my face in her hands. "What did those people do to you?"

"I'm okay, Mom," I said. I was still feeling traumatized by the experience, and I didn't want to start reliving all the details just yet. I wasn't sure if I would ever tell my mom that they had cut me open on an operating table without my even knowing what exactly they'd done. "I will tell you what happened," I continued. "But first I need you to meet someone."

I was sure that Hero would frighten them at first— especially my younger sisters—but I could not fight the urge to introduce them to my rescuer. Showing him to them would also help me to explain how I escaped from the hunters.

"Huh? Who?" my mother asked.

"Just put on some shoes and come with me," I said, tugging on her hand and leading her to the door.

My family followed me out of the house, and as we neared the square, my footsteps quickened. I felt oddly excited to introduce him to them, as though he were a dear friend. But when I turned the last corner and faced the square, I stopped dead in my tracks.

"What is it?" my family murmured behind me as they

arrived by my side.

"Hero," I breathed, my heart sinking as I gazed around the empty square. "He's gone."

CHAPTER 25: BEN

I wouldn't forget the promise that I'd made to myself after interrupting River's last dream.

I wouldn't haunt her after she no longer needed me.

After River turned the corner and headed back to her townhouse to see her family, I spread the griffin's wings and launched back into the air. Residents and visitors were still able to leave The Shade without permission, so I had no difficulty in rising outside of the boundary.

I could have left the beast on the island and traveled away in my spirit form, but without my control over him, this animal was dangerous. I had to lock him out of The Shade.

After breaching the invisible barrier and soaring away

from the island over the waves, it was time for me to let this griffin go. For good. I had pushed his body hard over the last few days. So hard, in fact, I'd been afraid that he might collapse mid-journey. I hadn't stopped once to feed him, or given him anything to drink. But his body seemed built to weather discomfort and hardship.

I raised my spirit out of him and watched as he staggered in the air. His wings stopped beating completely for a moment and he hurtled downward. Coming to his senses at the last second, just before he fell into the ocean, he flapped his wings and rose again in the sky. He paused, taking in his surroundings uncertainly, before launching into the direction opposite from The Shade.

"So long, Hero," I muttered, even as my chest twinged at the reminder of River.

I wasn't sure where he would go. But I had freed him from the hunters' grasp, and I supposed that wherever he ended up would at least be better than that.

I couldn't imagine what the creature must have been feeling. How odd it must have been for him, to be possessed like that for days... Then again, I'd experienced my own fair share of possession when the Elder had still had me under his influence. Though, thanks to Arron's vial of blue liquid, Basilius had never had the chance to control me completely.

My thoughts slowly turned back to the present. The waiting, inescapable present.

What do I do now?

As afraid as I'd been when River had been captured by the hunters, having my mind overtaken by her plight had actually been a kind of blessing in disguise for me. I'd been so consumed in figuring out how to rescue her that I hadn't had a lot of time to think about myself. Now that I did, I felt vacant.

I drifted to the nearby islet, the same one Jeramiah had brought my parents and grandfather to, and slumped down on a rock. I gazed out at the horizon. Dawn was breaking. A brilliant, breathtaking dawn. For a moment, I let its beauty overtake me as I listened to the sloshing of the waves against the rocks. In the distance, The Shade's birds awakened in their nests, and the redwood trees whispered. Engulfed in the calm and stillness of the morning, thoughts about my life and my fate ebbed away for a while.

My mind trailed back to the hunters. I felt shaken by everything I'd witnessed in their lair, and I still didn't know their goals or the purpose of their strange activities and operations. They were rumored to be backed by the government now, but I could only guess what their game plan was. Whatever it might be, I couldn't help but feel that nothing good would come of it.

Though of course, I couldn't exactly blame them. With more and more supernaturals filtering down from the supernatural dimension into the human realm, Earth's future was uncertain. Who knew what the future held? Who knew how much longer it would be until there wasn't a single human of sound mind left in the world who could deny the existence of supernaturals? Thanks to my misadventure in Chile, the code of secrecy had been broken and since then, there had been a number of other televised incidents. And no doubt those would only continue to increase. I foresaw a time when humans could no longer brush the events off as hoaxes. A time when this realm became so rife with paranormal creatures that encounters would become an everyday occurrence for regular citizens. Something they'd either have to live with, or fight against.

My mind reeled as I wondered what would really become of Earth if the balance tipped. Would the different species figure out a way to cohabitate? I guessed these matters were what the hunters were considering at present. Their actions, however strange and mysterious they appeared to be now, would in time become clear.

It was a chilling thought that whatever fate lay ahead for the world, I might have no choice but to be a passive spectator.

I stilled my mind again before I could sink back into despondency, my attention refocusing on the glowing horizon. As the minutes passed, the radiant ball of fire lifted higher and higher until it rose up fully from behind the waves. And it brought with it... an unexpected sense of comfort. As hopeless as my situation seemed, each day was a new beginning. Who knew exactly what the future held for me? Maybe it wouldn't be as hopeless as I feared. Maybe I wouldn't end up like Ernest, six hundred years from now sitting in some dingy guesthouse, wedded to the fantasies of strangers. Maybe the universe had something else in store for me. I didn't know what now, but hadn't I at least made some progress? I'd discovered that I could inhabit animals. I wasn't wholly locked out of the physical world... though I didn't believe I could ever be wholly in it. Barely even partially in it.

What kind of life can one live through an animal?

I wasn't sure where I belonged now. My soul still felt bound to my home, The Shade, as though I were tied to it by some invisible tether. But I needed to leave, at least for a while. I needed to try to discover more about this strange half-life.

I felt another pang as I thought of River. Of the last

interaction I'd had with her. She'd planted a gentle kiss on the griffin's face, and I'd been able to feel it. Then she'd hurried away, but glanced over her shoulder before turning the corner, allowing me to take in her beautiful face, her deep turquoise gaze, one last time.

At least I wasn't concerned about her and my family's safety any more. Jeramiah and his witch were out of The Shade now, and I doubted the island would have any more intruders ever again after the extreme measures they were putting into place. With the already strong presence of the dragons, they were making the island a fortress. They didn't need me hanging around to play security guard—and a rather useless one at that.

I leaned my head back and gazed up at the heavens.

My spirit isn't made for this world, this human dimension… and maybe not even the supernatural realm either. I'm here by artificial means alone. The thought chilled me, and I instinctively wanted to repel it, but… I couldn't help but wonder what Arron had really meant that night he'd handed me the vial of blue liquid that would keep me in this world.

"There is a place beyond death for all of us, whether we be humans, or supernaturals… But most aren't willing to find out," the Hawk had told me.

What is that place where spirits naturally go after death?

Those who don't stay behind?

I didn't have the first clue. Arron had been so cryptic that evening, and I hadn't been brought up in any particular faith or religion, so I had no pre-formed beliefs of my own.

There was only thing that I could assume:

It was somewhere far, far away.

Chapter 26: Derek

Thoughts of my nephew still weighed heavily on my mind, even as I went about organizing a complete overhaul of the island's security. My disappointment in him was fast turning to anger. But the strange thing was, as livid as I was with him for what he'd done to Kailyn, I felt almost madder for a different reason.

Why did he have to turn out like a carbon copy of my brother? Why couldn't he be even a little bit original?

I just couldn't let the thought go that we could have come to an understanding with Jeramiah. Even if we didn't become close, we could have parted on agreeable terms. It would have been symbolic of a reconciliation I'd never gotten with my brother and father, whose unceremonious departures from this world still hit a nerve in me even after all these years.

Still, I was accustomed to having a lot on my mind while still being forced to go about the runnings of the island. Within a matter of days, I had not only rid The Shade of the mermaid infestation, but also instituted a whole new set of rigid security procedures—procedures that, with hindsight, we should have introduced years ago, but which we'd always ended up putting off due to not only members of my Council, but also a high proportion of our citizens, protesting over what a severe inconvenience it would be to all of us. Jeramiah's antics, however, had been the final straw. I didn't even bother to consult the Council. I had a brief discussion with Sofia before relaying my orders.

It had actually been with the dragons' help, rather than our witches', that we had finally freed our shores of the merfolk threat. The thought had occurred to me to ask if the fire-breathers enjoyed the taste of mer-flesh. Jeriad, whose eye had recovered thanks to Ibrahim's expertise, had informed me that many of them had never tasted it before, but all of them were willing to give it a go. And so, a horde of about fifty dragons shifted into their beastly forms and dipped into the ocean. As creatures of fire, I hadn't known if they liked water, but it didn't seem to bother them—*"Water is fine. It's ice that we despise,"* Jeriad had informed me.

The dragons swam through the waves, their long, scaly backs and tails reminding me of crocodiles as they floated near the water's surface. Within the space of a day, the dragons had circled the island dozens of times and by the time night fell, they confirmed that every single merfolk had either been eaten or fled for fear of their lives. Each of the dragons even thanked me personally for suggesting such a delicacy as they emerged from the ocean and returned to their mountain chambers. Now we could raise the temporary boundary that had lined our beaches and prevented entrance to the water, though of course, the main boundary that enclosed the island along with its immediate surrounding waters would remain, stronger than ever.

Once these most urgent matters had been seen to, my mind returned, predictably, to my nephew.

Jeramiah, Jeramiah, Jeramiah.

I was growing sick of his name flitting through my head, and yet still I couldn't drop the subject. Perhaps it was due to the pent-up frustration I felt over my own son, being able to do nothing to help him in his plight—wherever Ben was now. Sofia and I had interfered before in an attempt to help him, but all signs indicated that we'd only made his situation worse. And so, Jeramiah continued to haunt my mind.

At first I'd feared that my nephew had kidnapped River, rather than the hunters, and that her capture would be yet another strike against his character. But then Corrine came hurrying to Sofia and me to inform us that River had returned safely and that it had indeed been the hunters who'd managed to swipe her. I was anxious to hear her story, but there would be time for that later, once she was rested.

As I brooded over my nephew, I left the spare room in Vivienne's penthouse, where Sofia and I were staying until we rebuilt a new penthouse of our own. It was as I walked along the forest path, deep in thought, that an odd idea struck me.

I should talk to Claudia.

***

As I rapped on the door of Yuri and Claudia's penthouse, it was a strange feeling to be visiting the blonde vixen for advice. Throughout all the centuries we'd known each other, this was a first.

But she'd known my brother better than anyone. Hers was always the bed he'd fallen into whenever he wanted an escape, and I suspected that it was with her he'd shared the most about himself. Likely far more than he'd ever revealed even to our father.

Jeramiah's accusation of me, that I'd never taken the trouble to get to know Lucas, did hold a thread of truth. We had never been close, and I had never really understood him. But I had never been the one to instigate fights. I had always tried to resolve conflicts like gentlemen. It had been him who'd closed himself off from me, even as I'd tried to get through to him. I had given up on him in the end. He'd worn me down.

I was shaken from my thoughts as Yuri opened the door. His eyes widened as he laid eyes on me. "Derek? What's going on? Come in, come in."

I followed him through the door and into the hallway.

Claudia—and her protruding belly—emerged from the kitchen carrying a bowl of roasted peanuts, her mouth bulging with the snack.

I still hadn't gotten used to seeing Claudia as a human. It was hard to believe that the pregnant woman standing before me now—a soon-to-be mother—was the same bloodthirsty creature who had tortured Benjamin Hudson and countless other male slaves senseless.

"What's up, King Derek?" she asked.

I took a seat on the couch and coughed my throat clear. "I'm here to see you actually, Claudia. I want to ask you for... uh, some advice."

Claudia's eyes immediately brightened. I was certain that if she were to write a list of three things she loved most in the world, it would consist of Yuri, her baby, and the sound of her own voice. "What about?" she asked, slinking onto the sofa next to me.

"About my brother. Lucas."

Claudia frowned. "A bit late for advice about ol' Lucas, don't you think?"

"Well, actually it's more about his son, Jeramiah..." I breathed out in frustration before proceeding to recap the whole conversation I'd had with him on the rock, as well as the desire I held for reconciliation.

When I'd finished, Claudia looked lost in thought as she munched on her peanuts.

"Hmm," she murmured. "So you don't want Jeramiah to become another wayward satellite like your brother was."

"I guess that sums it up," I muttered, slumping against the backrest and folding my arms over my chest. "I'm honestly not sure what I hope to achieve by telling you this. I just thought, since you knew Lucas better than any of us..." My voice trailed off as I glanced at Claudia.

"I hear you, Derek. I hear you. You did the right thing in coming to me for advice..." She paused to put her now-empty bowl down on the coffee table before dusting her hands off and crossing her legs. She turned to face me fully. "You really wanna know what I think?" she asked, quirking a brow.

"What?"

"That boy just needs some good lovin'."

I could hardly have expected a different answer from Claudia. I caught Yuri rolling his eyes… and so did she.

"What?" Claudia admonished her husband.

Yuri chuckled. "Continue, Doctor. Didn't mean to interrupt your flow."

She stood up, hands on her hips. "Well don't *you* think he needs loving?" she shot at him. "He's an orphan, you know."

Yuri shrugged. "I guess it's kind of hard to feel a lot of sympathy for a cold-blooded murderer."

Now it was Claudia's turn to roll her eyes. "And what was I, when you professed your undying love for me? What was I, when you proposed?"

That silenced Yuri. Claudia had been one of the vampires who'd indulged in her dark side the most. I'd no idea how many innocent humans she'd tortured to death. I was sure even she'd lost count.

Claudia turned on me. "That was the problem with Lucas. He never got any good loving."

I heaved a sigh, half wondering why I was even asking, "And what exactly do you classify as 'good loving'?"

"Firm love. Unconditional love. Unrelenting love. Even... forced love."

I raised a brow. "Would you care to clarify?"

"I'm the best example. I spent centuries trying to escape from this guy"—she jabbed a finger at Yuri—"but he wouldn't leave me alone. He loved me even when I shoved him away. Even when I deliberately set out to hurt him. His love wasn't conditioned by how I responded to him. He loved me without bounds... and eventually, he cracked me." Claudia paused, her cheeks flushed with passion as she gazed at Yuri.

Yuri's cheeks had flushed a little, too, as he gazed adoringly back at her. Despite their banter and bickering, their love for one another ran deeper than most couples could ever hope for.

"Well," I said, breaking the span of silence after Claudia's speech, "I doubt there's a female counterpart of Yuri hanging around and waiting for Jeramiah."

"Augh," Claudia groaned, throwing her hands in the air. *Drama queen.* "You're missing the point, Derek! Good loving doesn't only take place between lovers. Unconditional love can be given to anyone, whoever you are. Between brother and sister. Father and son. Uncle and nephew. Geez, do you get the hint already?"

There was a pause as I gazed at Claudia with a slight frown on my face.

What she was saying made sense, and yet I still couldn't see how her advice could apply in Jeramiah's case. Yes, unconditional love could take place between anybody. But I didn't love Jeramiah as an uncle would, nor as a father would. He was more like... unfinished business that I needed to cross off my bucket list.

Yuri ended up voicing my doubt for me, apparently following the same train of thought: "But you can't manufacture love, Claudia. I loved you because... dammit, I just couldn't help it. But why would Derek love Jeramiah? He barely even knows the bastard, and the little Derek does know of him is enough to make Derek hate him forever."

"Firstly," Claudia said, holding up a finger, "don't call Jeramiah a bastard. It's just this kind of labeling that played on Lucas' psyche. Yes, Lucas was an asshole, but the more people called him that and labeled him that way, the more entrenched in his behavior he became." She paused for a breath. Her eyes returned to me. "Secondly, Derek, that's where forced love comes in. If you really want to get through to Jeramiah, don't consider your own feelings. Just act unconditionally, and do what's best for him. You could also think of it as… tough love."

Tough love.

That sounded more interesting to me.

Much more interesting…

The first threads of a plan slowly formed in my mind. I stood up and gazed down in almost wonderment at Claudia. I couldn't have expected the encounter to be so enlightening.

Claudia's countenance brightened, and she grinned at me. "Well? What are you thinking?"

A faint smile spread across my lips. "I'm thinking that you ought to start charging for this."

Claudia's grin broadened. "I doubt you could afford me." She winked.

"Five kilos of peanuts an hour?" I offered, my heart feeling unusually light as I made my way to the front door.

"Oh, she eats way more than that," Yuri scoffed.

"Why don't you try lugging a watermelon around in your stomach?" I guessed Claudia would have shoved Yuri in the shoulder, but I didn't even turn around to see any more of their banter. After calling, "Thank you," over my shoulder, I hurried down the elevator and away from their treehouse.

As I raced through the trees, back toward Sofia's and my room in my sister's penthouse, more pieces of my plan fell into place until I had figured out what my first step had to be.

The time had finally come for me to turn back into the real Derek Novak. Back into the man who was feared for centuries by even his closest companions.

Back into a vampire.

Jeramiah wants a father. I can be a father to him...

The father of his nightmares.

Chapter 27: Julie

I didn't even know where to guide the dolphins. I just knew that Braithe and I had to get away. Far away.

Whatever had happened to Aisha, I was certain that she would make it her life's mission to hunt me down and give me the end she was so desperate to mete out. I doubted she would rest again until she'd watched me die a slow, painful death.

I felt paranoid now that we floated so exposed on the waves, out in the open for anyone to see. The boat had a small shelter, but it wasn't the same kind of protection I'd had from her while swimming deep underwater. If she was scouring the waves, she would spot us.

I urged the dolphins on, frustrated that this particular breed didn't possess the same speed as the sharks bound to my and the Mansons' ship.

Come on. Come on!

We'd traveled for hours when I caught sight of a huge landmass in the distance. I slowed the boat. I recognized this island. We were nearing the shores of the ogres' kingdom.

I despised these waters. Not only were they frequented by violent ogres, but they were filled with frightening creatures, just like those lethal crabs.

I began veering the dolphins in the opposite direction of the shoreline when a chilling thought struck me.

Where can I actually go to hide with Braithe?

I couldn't keep sailing the seas—we were far too vulnerable in this boat. I had to get us to land… but which land? The list of places that I could think of where I could escape alone was short enough, but with Braithe? The list became nonexistent. Who would want him on their island?

I had been in too much of a hurry to leave the witch's castle to bring the box with me, so I had nothing to hide him in either.

But on the shore of the ogres' kingdom… I knew that there was a gate leading back to the human realm. It led to an uninhabited tropical island, rumored to be not all that far from The Shade.

If I passed through that gate with Braithe, we could pass the rest of the day and night hidden somewhere on that small, deserted island. It felt safer than staying in the supernatural realm. I was sure that Aisha would be less likely to find us there.

Then in the morning… I wasn't sure what we would do. What we *could* do. But at least we'd be safer than we were now, and I'd have a chance to clear my mind and think about what our next step should be. I still hadn't given up hope of finding a cure. Arletta, Colin and Frederick might be lost forever, but I still had Braithe… *And Hans is still in Cruor.* Although Uma couldn't help me anymore, there had to be someone else in this universe who could.

I scanned the beach more carefully. I couldn't spot any ogres roaming it. If I hurried there now with Braithe, we could probably slip through the gate unnoticed.

My gaze roamed Braithe and then fell on the drawstring bag, filled with sedative-laced darts. I was certain that I had more than enough of the witch's drug to keep Braithe under control. And if I came up with a new plan quickly, we might only end up being in the human realm for a day or two… *I mean, what could go wrong?*

THE END IS NEAR...

Dear Shaddict,

Ben and River's journey will continue in *Book 23: A Flight of Souls* — the PENULTIMATE book in their story, leading up to the thrilling finale in Book 24.

Please visit: www.bellaforrest.net for details.

Here's a preview of the beautiful cover!

Thank you for reading.

Love,
Bella x

P.S. Join my VIP email list and I'll send you a personal reminder as soon as I have a new book out. Visit here to sign up: www.forrestbooks.com

(You'll also be the first to receive news about movies/TV show as well as other exciting projects coming up!)

P.P.S. Follow The Shade on Instagram and check out some of the beautiful graphics: @ashadeofvampire

You can also come say hi to me on Facebook: www.facebook.com/AShadeOfVampire

And Twitter: @ashadeofvampire

I'd love to hear from you.

Made in the USA
San Bernardino, CA
03 April 2016